AN INTRODUCTION TO
RITUAL MAGIC

Books by Dion Fortune with Gareth Knight

An Introduction to Ritual Magic
The Arthurian Formula
The Circuit of Force
The Magical Battle of Britain
Practical Occultism
Principles of Esoteric Healing
Principles of Hermetic Philosophy
Spiritualism and Occultism

Other books by Dion Fortune

Machinery of the Mind
The Esoteric Philosophy of Love and Marriage
The Psychology of the Servant Problem
The Soya Bean
The Esoteric Orders and their Work
The Problem of Purity
Sane Occultism
The Training and Work of an Initiate
Mystical Meditations on the Collects
Spiritualism in the Light of Occult Science
Psychic Self-Defence
Glastonbury - Avalon of the Heart
The Mystical Qabalah
Practical Occultism in Daily Life
The Cosmic Doctrine
Through the Gates of Death
Applied Magic
Aspects of Occultism

Occult Fiction

The Demon Lover
The Goat-Foot God
Moon Magic
The Sea Priestess
The Secrets of Dr Taverner
The Winged Bull

Other books by Gareth Knight

Dion Fortune and the Inner Light
Esoteric Training in Everyday Life
Evoking the Goddess (*aka* The Rose Cross and the Goddess)
Experience of the Inner Worlds
Granny's Magic Cards
Magic and the Western Mind (*aka* A History of White Magic)
Magical Images and the Magical Imagination
The Magical World of the Inklings
The Magical World of the Tarot
Merlin and the Grail Tradition
The Occult: an Introduction
Occult Exercises and Practices
The Practice of Ritual Magic
A Practical Guide to Qabalistic Symbolism
The Secret Tradition in Arthurian Legend
Tarot and Magic (*aka* The Treasure House of Images)

AN INTRODUCTION TO RITUAL MAGIC

by
DION FORTUNE
and
GARETH KNIGHT

THOTH PUBLICATIONS
Loughborough, Leicestershire.

Details of the "Work and Aims" of the Society of the Inner Light,
founded by Dion Fortune, may be obtained by writing
(with postage please) to the Secretariat at
38 Steele's Road, London NW3 4RG

A CIP catalogue record for this book
is available from the British Library.

ISBN 978-1-870450-26-3

Cover design by Helen Surman
Printed and bound in Great Britain

Published by Thoth Publications
64 Leopold Street, Loughborough, LE11 5DN
Web Address: www.thoth.co.uk
email: enquiries@thoth.co.uk

DEDICATION

to D.C. and Sr. I.N.C.
to whom also my thanks

G.K.

CONTENTS

INTRODUCTION

Dion Fortune's Introduction to Ritual Magic first appeared, like other of her books, as separate articles in "The Inner Light Magazine", the journal that she founded and edited during the inter-war years. These articles were then collected together by me in my alter ego as editor of *New Dimensions* magazine and run as a series in 1963/5. It gives me great pleasure to see them at last given birth in volume form.

Of all her writings this dissertation on the techniques of ritual magic strikes me as being as fresh and to the point as the day it was written. Indeed it is not the esoteric content that betrays the passing of years but references made to everyday life. Thus pound notes no longer exist, and if they did it is doubtful if the Bank of England would pass gold across the counter in exchange for one. And modern marketing and production techniques in the dairy industry make it unlikely that we find a hair of the cow in a bottle of milk. Whilst gramophones have given place to record and CD players and sound systems of various types.

I have not presumed to edit out any of these contemporary references, still less to try to rephrase Dion Fortune's use of the masculine pronoun to indicate members of the human race of either gender.

My own contribution to this volume is one of amplification rather than amendment. To each of the chapters provided by Dion Fortune I have added one of my own under the same title. This, in some respects, may prove to be something of a commentary on points of difference or detail, but in the main my attempt has been to fill in some of the applications that Dion Fortune, writing in her day, would have felt reluctant to include.

The veil of occult secrecy has been rolled back a considerable way over the past sixty years and I hope that I have succeeded in rounding out Dion Fortune's pioneer work to provide the kind of explicit and practical text that she herself would, I think, have provided if she were writing today.

In this I have been enormously helped by my daughter Rebecca, whose contribution demonstrates to me that the torch of initiation burns as brightly as ever it did, and that old inner plane friends and teachers can span the generations. Old soldiers never die, as the old song says, but there is one we know who will not even fade away!

GARETH KNIGHT

Chapter 1a

TYPES OF MIND WORKING
Dion Fortune

Occultism is the study of certain little-understood powers of the human mind and of the mind side of Nature. Its pursuit, therefore, depends upon the possession of the capacity to make use of these little-understood powers of the human mind and to perceive the mind side of Nature.

The first step in the pursuit of practical occultism is to train the mind. Until this is done we are not in a position to make a start. Everything, therefore, must wait upon the acquirement of the necessary faculties.

Only a very small portion of occult work is concerned with supernormal phenomena that can be perceived by the physical senses, and these phenomena play no part in the very valuable practical applications to life and its problems of which occult science is capable and which constitute its great value to mankind. The occurrence of such phenomena depends upon the presence of a materialising medium; such mediums are rare, and their right use requires great skill and experience. The major part of occultism, and all the most practical part, depends upon the possession of some degree at least of sensitiveness or psychism for its appreciation.

Now psychism, when we come to examine it, is really hyper-sensitiveness, and all of us are sensitive in varying degrees, perhaps more so than we realise. This sensitiveness enables us to perceive subtle influences that pass unnoticed in the hurly-burly of the physical senses. We are receiving these impressions all the time, and we are registering them subconsciously, and being influenced by them in varying degrees. This is normal to all human beings.

The difference between the psychic and the average person is that the psychic is able to perceive consciously what the average person only perceives subconsciously.

Psychism is due to various causes, and should be classified and dealt with accordingly. Firstly, we get the natural psychic, whose temperament is so sensitive that subtle vibrations are perceptible to him. Life in the workaday world is to him what life in a tornado would be to other people. He is caught up and whirled about by the roaring vortex about him; he has no place to lay his head nor any rest for his foot. Unless he can find some means of insulating or protecting himself, normality is impossible for him. Many nervous invalids owe their illness to this cause.

Normal persons under severe stress occasionally get into this condition temporarily. Exhaustion brought about by abstention from food and emotional strain sometimes give rise to it. There are also certain drugs which will induce it.

There is a certain type of psychic training which combines breathing exercises with abstention from flesh foods and the vibrations of certain sounds. Various types of this method, which comes to us from the East, have been adapted for Western students. It is not, in my opinion, a method to be advised because, even in the hands of an experienced guru, it is not without risks. Practised without the supervision of a guru, or under the guidance of a guru who has had no experience in handling European pupils, the results can be disastrous.

Moreover, it is never wise to hyper-sensitise oneself unless one is in the happy position of being able to control the conditions in which one lives. Sensitising techniques, therefore, should never be employed save by persons of leisure and private means. They are certainly not for those who have to earn a living in a competitive world.

Secondly, we get the type of psychism which is produced by the ability to cut out the sense-impressions at will, so that the subtle vibrations are perceived. A psychic of this type is like a person who stops the gramophone in order to be able to hear what is being said on the telephone.

This kind of psychism depends for its efficacy upon the possession, in a very high degree, of the power to concentrate. It is a satisfactory method because it also confers the power, so necessary to any psychic, of being able to close down the subtle senses at will. It is a laborious method both to acquire and to use, however, and demands prolonged and arduous training.

A third type of psychism consists in holding the mind perfectly still and "listening" to the impressions that arise in it. This is the simplest method to acquire, but it is also the least dependable, for it is very difficult to get entirely away from our preconceived ideas, and in any matter in which our feelings are involved it is totally unreliable.

The fourth type of psychism is that of induced vision. This method avails itself of the natural psychism of the subconscious mind, and employs a technique to render the subconscious content visible to consciousness and then interpret it.

But although these four types of psychism can be distinguished, psychism of a mixed kind is almost invariably employed in actual practice; for it is found that the employment of a technique which renders the subconscious content available tends to increase the natural sensitiveness, and so give its practitioner a foothold in class one. A certain degree of concentration such as is employed in the second type is necessary in order to produce an induced vision that sticks to the point and conveys anything intelligible; and in order to enable the vision to formulate, something of the third type of technique is necessary.

The best type of psychism, which combines the widest range with the greatest concentration, and which has what chemists call the minimum toxicity, that is to say, which produces least disturbance of normal consciousness, is obtained by a technique which avails itself of something from all these methods in varying proportions; for according to a well-understood pharmaceutical law, the actions of certain drugs reinforce each other, and they are far more effectual when blended than when taken separately.

We need to aim at power of concentration combined with sensitivity, and the development of skill in the technique which enables us to make the subconscious content available to consciousness.

First and foremost, however, must be the power of concentration, for it is that, and that alone which gives mind control. Concentration is the power to pay attention to one thing at a time and to refuse to be distracted. People possess it in varying degrees. It is said of Sir Isaac Newton that he continued his calculations after his papers had caught on fire, oblivious of the flames that were singeing his wig; while at the other end of the scale is the deranged person whose mind attends to nothing but is distracted by every impression.

The power to concentrate, granted a normal mind, is largely a matter of habit and responds readily to practice. For its cultivation we use the same method that we would employ for the development of the muscles – regular, graduated exercise. To demand of the person unaccustomed to study a prolonged and concentrated attention is to demand of him what he is incapable of giving. To demand of him that he shall consider one idea for five minutes is to demand of him what he can do if he chooses to take the trouble. He may have to take a good deal of trouble at first, if he is a scatter-brained person, unaccustomed to use his mind, but by the time he has repeated the operation on half a dozen consecutive days he will find that he can do the exercise without effort, and is beginning to lengthen the time spontaneously.

There are a great many tricks and short cuts in the art of managing the mind. For instance, it is much easier to "meditate" than to "contemplate". Therefore one learns meditation before one attempts contemplation. In meditation the mind follows a train of thought that circles round a central idea. In contemplation one excludes everything else from one's mind and just looks at the central idea, allowing it to expand and fill one's whole being. One cannot still the mind in contemplation until one has learnt to steady it in meditation.

Again, it is much easier to meditate on concrete ideas than upon abstract ones; therefore one practises meditation exercises upon common objects such as a penny or a piece of coal before attempting those spiritual exercises that exalt consciousness.

A great many books have been written about mind-training, and many of them are very useful so far as the rudiments of the work go, but they have their limitations. It is possible to train the surface of the mind by systems taken out of books, and to improve the memory and powers of attention; but it is not possible to open up the higher consciousness except under skilled guidance.

There are three ways in which the mind works, as we shall readily see if we observe it. Most commonly we think in words and in series of picture images like a cinematograph film. But there is a third and higher type of mentality, and which comes occasionally to all of us at times of stress. This is a thinking in terms of pure idea, in which the idea arises in the mind complete and does not have to be thought out, but comes as a flash of realisation which we apprehend in a sudden glimpse of insight and then gradually unfold and realise in all its implications. If we examine ourselves we shall find that we have probably had experience in varying proportions of all three types of mentation.

The physical culturist, when he exercises, takes first one group of muscles and then another and makes special use of them, exerting them to their fullest capacity. Likewise when we train the mind we get the best results if we pick out a faculty at a time and concentrate on it. There are special ways of exercising each faculty. We train the audile imagination, as the power to think in words is called, by giving imaginary lectures for five minutes on simple subjects with which we are familiar, imagining we hear ourselves speaking. We train the visual imagination, as the interior cinematograph film is called, by calling up before the mind's eye a series of pictures of some familiar walk as we should see them if we were treading that very path. With a little practice we can learn to do both these things with a very remarkable degree of vividness.

People usually incline to be either audile or visual in their type of mind-working, just as they are either right- or left-handed, but a little effort will usually enable them to acquire the type that is not their chosen one, just as we can learn to use the left hand for things usually done by the right. It is only a matter of effort at the start, one soon acquires the knack, for the mind is mainly a creature of habit.

People who are given to day-dreaming and fantasy find little difficulty in this exercise, which they have really practised unawares for years. All they have to learn is to direct their aimless romancing to useful purposes. Day-dreaming is supposed to be a very debilitating thing for the brain, according to orthodox psychologists; and so it can be if indulged in over-much or injudiciously. It has, however, a very important place in the technique of mind-working; the same place, in fact, that is occupied by the architect's plan in the building of a house. Therefore to condemn the use of the imagination in romancing is as foolish as to accuse the sketching, scribbling architect of wasting his time and bid him get busy with a barrow if he wants to do something useful.

This image building, done with knowledge by means of the skilled use of the imagination, plays the chief part in mind-work. This is a thing which is very little understood, either by psychologists or occultists. It has a twofold importance, both subjective and objective; both in mind-training and in magic.

Its importance in mind-training is insufficiently realised, because those who teach mind-training systems, whether from the standpoint of esoteric development or business efficiency, always seem to have a very old-fashioned concept of psychology, and go to work as if the conscious mind were all there is inside our skulls, which is very far from being the case. Coué was on the right track, but he stopped just short of the top of the hill. If he had employed the visual imagination to make pictures as well as the audile imagination to formulate the words "Every day in every way I get better and better", he would have re-discovered one of the ancient keys to the Mysteries.

He realised very clearly that it is useless to try and drive the subconscious mind by the brute force of the conscious will applied to its surface. This is a fact that stands out in the experience of everyone who has made the attempt. On the basis of this experience Coué formulated his Law of Reversed Effort, which is but a restatement in psychological terms of St. Paul's experience, "The good I would I do not, and the evil I would not, that I do." Because Coué observed this reaction, he discarded the effort of the directed will altogether, and in fact advised against its use. Now this may be well enough when we are attempting a physical healing. For it is apt to produce negative auto-suggestion when, after having repeated the magic words, "Every day in every way I get better and better" the requisite number of times, we try to get out of bed and find that we are not any better. Physical healings take time if they are genuinely physical and not neurotic. These things do not work like Abracadabra except in fiction, and in that class of "uplifting" literature to which that term might unkindly but not untruly be applied.

When it comes to dealing with the breaking or forming of habits, the development of capacity, other work of character building, to all of which auto-suggestion is readily applicable and of the greatest value, the will can with advantage be used to reinforce the auto-suggestion. If, for instance, one applied auto-suggestion to learning to skate, or any other achievement of physical skill, one would not make very much progress if one contented oneself with saying, "Every day in every way I skate better and better," and then remained seated beside the rink. If, however, as one staggers onto the ice one repeats this formula instead of the more popular one, "I know I'm going to fall. I know I'm going to fall", the results are very encouraging. True, one must expect to sit down hard occasionally in the early stages, and a cynic has even said that skates should be sold in sets of three, and not in pairs; but a wise man has also said that the coward dies a thousand times, but the brave man only dies once. A coward, be it noted, is usually an imaginative person.

Personally, I do not believe the Law of Reversed Effort to be a true formulation of subconscious resistance. Like the rest of us, the subconscious mind is set in its ways, that is all. It is not deliberately spiteful towards the conscious mind as Coué would have us believe. It has its own ideas as to the best way of getting us what we want, and these ideas are apt to be short-sighted, or what Jung calls infantile, for the subconscious mind has its limitations and modern education passes it by and leaves it illiterate. The subconscious mind often has a much shrewder notion of what we really want than we are prepared to admit even to ourselves, and like the poacher's dog, responds to the pitch of the voice and not to the actual command, and when bidden to come to heel, dives down the rabbit hole.

The subconscious mind, however, although its education is so widely neglected, is by no means the imbecile it is generally represented to be. Approached in the right way, it is, like the rest of us, exceedingly responsive. But there is an old saying that a nod is as good as a wink to a blind horse, and when we talk to our own subconscious minds in a language they do not understand, we get the same paucity of results that occurs when we apply the same method to other people's conscious minds. If we remember how we ourselves feel when a foreigner makes an eloquent appeal to us in his own tongue, we shall know how the subconscious mind feels when the usual methods of mind training are applied to it. It can make neither head nor tail of the commands that are being dinned into its ears, and if pressed too hard, may turn nasty.

The only way to talk to the subconscious mind is through the pictorial imagination. It has a very archaic mode of mentation that developed before speech had been thought of. It is unresponsive to logic, or argument, or appeals to its better nature, just as a deaf man is unresponsive, and for the same reason. But show it a picture, and it understands and is only too ready to cooperate now that it knows what is required of it.

Not realising this fact, we are constantly showing our subconscious minds the wrong kind of pictures. This is the real key to the Law of Reversed Effort; the misunderstood instruction, not the innate cussedness of the subconscious, as Coué would have us believe. It is really an exemplification of the older and better known maxim that the hand follows the eye. If you look over the hedge when driving a car, you will end in the ditch because, all unconsciously, you will steer in the direction in which you are looking. The novice keeps his eye on the kerb in order to avoid running into it, and follows St. Paul's example by doing the thing he would not. The expert looks where he wants to go, and gets there. If you keep your eye on the tip of your near side mudguard you will infallibly drive in a circle. Knowing this fact as we do by common experience, and having had it pointed out to us by Coué, it is strange that applied psychology, whether in the form of mind training or psychotherapy, makes so little use of it.

Magistrates know that gangster films produce a crop of gangster crimes in the districts where they are shown, and express themselves in good round terms on the subject. Boys see these films, day-dream the plots with themselves in the place of the hero; character deteriorates, and juvenile delinquency is the result. Supposing we indulged habitually in fantasies of a different type, might not the result be something quite different from delinquency?

This is what the initiate does in the visions he induces by means of invocation and contemplation. This is a part, and an important part, of the techniques of the Mysteries, but it must be used intelligently and with understanding if it is not to do us more harm than good.

The uninstructed person thinks he is developing psychism when he sees elves, archangels, and elementals with the inner eye. The instructed person knows that he is using a technique of the imagination in order to clothe with visible form intangible things that would otherwise be imperceptible to his consciousness. He knows that it is a form of visual auto-suggestion, as distinguished from Coué's audile auto-suggestion. He makes use of it for two reasons, first, because it is the most effectual way of handling the levels of the mind that are beyond the direct access of normal consciousness. He uses it, in fact, for its auto-suggestive value, and not as an end in itself, and this is the way it should be used if we do not want the auto-suggestive effect to get out of hand and end in hallucination.

He is therefore neither credulous nor sceptical concerning the picture psychism that presents itself to his mind in the course of his occult work. He is not credulous, because he knows its real significance as a mode of mind working, and therefore does not take it at its face value. He is not sceptical, because although he does not regard the images perceived as real in themselves, he knows that they represent realities that are of value to him. No-one makes the mistake of thinking that a pound note has any intrinsic value, but everyone knows that if he were to present it at the Bank of England, he could obtain a pound's worth of gold for it. So it is with visionary psychism. If we interpret it, we find it has a genuine significance, but it also has no intrinsic value in such things as we understand as phenomenal existence.

The student, therefore, learns the skilled technical use of the visual imagination; the initiate learns to interpret the visions and to exchange the pound note of fantasy for metaphysical gold.

Chapter 1b

TYPES OF MIND WORKING
Gareth Knight

In most forms of practical occultism we are dealing with what Dion Fortune likes to call "certain little-understood powers of the human mind" although many of these powers are more common than we generally suppose. It is really a matter of analysing what our various mind powers and levels are and then deliberately cultivating them by various forms of training and technique.

Powers of psychism are by no means as rare as is generally assumed. They are simply a particular use of the human imagination, and we all of us possess an imagination, whether or not we choose to use it in a constructive fashion.

Most of us put up some kind of mental block when the word 'psychism' is used, and assume that when a psychic vision is described it is rather after the fashion of a luminous mist building up before us, in a corner of the room or at a sacred site. That it is a discernible "out there" – by means of some rare faculty of the physical eye that some gifted people possess and others do not. We may thus go around peering in various directions with eyes half closed hoping to "see" some external or semi external manifestation in this way.

Invariably we are disappointed, which is to our advantage. For indeed if we were not disappointed, then we ought to have cause to be alarmed, for externally seen or heard psychic perceptions are of the order of exteriorised delirium and hallucination. That is to say, evidence of psychopathology rather than subtle powers of the mind.

The precise external or internal reality of "astral forms", and the philosophical and psychological conclusions to be drawn therefrom, will be considered later. For our immediate practical purposes let us state quite plainly that psychism, whether of images seen with the inner eye, or words or music heard with the inner ear, is a matter of the imagination - and of the controlled use of the imagination at that.

There is, we have to say, no shortage of examples of the uncontrolled use of the imagination within the occult movement. For occultism, like the arts, is a discipline that depends very much upon the use of the imagination, and this means that it attracts more than its share of the immature, the pretentious and the self-deluded.

The development of any talent is no easy process. Just as the creative artist needs to serve a long apprenticeship to develop the necessary technique to bring the powers of creative expression to full development, so does the occultist (ritual magician or otherwise), have to undergo a similar process – and many are the false trails and false dawns upon the way.

However, all of us possess the necessary basic skills within our psychological make-up. The imagination is a common heritage, as are all the other mental faculties that make us into human beings.

In different men or women, such is the diversity of human character, all of our faculties and talents may be present in different proportions and may be applied in different ways. This may be a result of genetic inheritance, family and social background, or individual psychology. None of us however are totally devoid of any natural human faculty, despite the fact that it is possible to over-express or to repress certain of them to some extent.

Let us make a list of the various faculties of the human being. This can clarify our ideas, and present us with a plan for action, as long as we do not turn this simple basic structure into mentally constricting water tight compartments.

Tradition tends to try to analyse life into sets of seven. Seven days of the week, seven notes in the diatonic scale. These are man made conventions and work none the less well for that, although they tend to break down when applied to objective physical reality, as in the ancient classification of seven planets. But the seven fold convention runs deeply within our psychology and one reason for this may be that the inner worlds are so constructed, giving us an intuitive tendency to project this form onto the outer world.

Even the pioneering physicist Isaac Newton thought in terms of seven when he came to describe the colours of the rainbow, though close observation of the spectrum does not readily reveal seven distinct and separate colours. There are more like six, with various indefinable graduations between them.

Anyhow, if we apply a similar convention to the spectrum of human consciousness we could come up with something like the list below:

1. Spiritual will
2. Moral conscience
3. Intuitions
4. Rational mind
5. Idealistic emotions
6. Instinctive emotions
7. Physical body and its electro-magnetic matrix

It would be possible to make other divisions, but they would be broadly similar, just as we might describe the rainbow in slightly different terms to the conventional red - orange - yellow - green - blue - indigo - violet.

We could further divide it into a more general three-fold structure and various schools of elementary occult thought have their own preferred nomenclature.

Thus the spiritual will, moral conscience and intuitions can be regarded as the faculties of the Higher Self or Individuality, (which some schools also call the Soul or the Evolutionary Personality). Whilst the rational mind and higher and lower emotions are those of the Lower Self or Personality (also known as the Incarnationary Personality, and to St.Paul as "the flesh"). Note that all share the physical body as a mode of expression within the physical world, and it is a common misunderstanding to assume that it was only the physical body and its appetites that St Paul meant when he referred to the flesh.

The physical body is also something rather more than a carcass, devoid of life. When a physical body does become a carcass it immediately starts to obey a different set of laws and circumstances and begins to decay. Whilst it is maintained in being by the higher or inner structures of the electro-magnetic and etheric energies of what are sometimes called the sub-planes of the physical, then it remains as a vehicle for conscious and intelligent life expression that has its roots in all and any of the higher faculties, from spiritual will to instinctive reactions.

Bear in mind that we all of us have all these faculties, even if some of them may seem dormant. It would be a mistake to think that a very materialistically minded and selfishly motivated personality has no higher self even if the latter's sense of spiritual responsibility and destiny, moral conscience or intuitions are ignored or seldom acted upon. In after death conditions the balance will be restored, and this accounts for the general tradition in various religions of the existence of a post-mortem personal judgement, and purgation or purification, and destruction of all that is spiritually false or corrupt, whether in medieval hell fire or in the maw of Amemait, the ancient Egyptian "devourer" god, part lion, part hippopotamus, part crocodile.

What concerns us is how all of these faculties within the complete human being may be brought into as full a function as possible, and then used in a magical way.

This first aim, of developing our inherent faculties, is very much the province of psychotherapeutic and self-development courses. It is a worthy aim in itself, which can lead to greater fulfilment, usefulness and self expression in life, and there are many books and courses devoted to this end.

Our aim, however, goes further than that, for ritual magic is a specialisation that not only strives to develop these faculties, but to use them in a particular direction, and that direction lies in opening up awareness to inner levels of creation and being able to function thereon.

This is not the same as the psychology of self or spiritual development. It comprises the other half of Dion Fortune's definition of occultism. That is to say, not only "the study of certain little-understood powers of the human mind" but also *"of the mind side of Nature"*.

This "mind side of Nature" is by no means a subjective or introverted state. It comprises the whole objective mechanism of intelligent consciousness that lies behind every manifestation of physical life; that is to say behind every animal, organism, plant, stone, planet, star, mineral, gem, landscape, from the smallest sub-atomic particle to the greatest galactic system. Just as the physical body of man is the vehicle of an interior life, so, according to this world view, all other physical bodies are expressions of different kinds and levels of intelligence.

This means that the universe didn't just "happen" - either by big bang or long evolution - or by a combination of the two. If there was a big bang, it was the intelligent FIAT LUX, "Let there be Light" of the Creator. If there was subsequent evolution in space and time this was the work of created consciousnesses of various kinds, of swarms of spirits, creative sparks from the divine fire, be they Elohim, or human, angelic or elemental creatures, or whatever other category of being that may exist within or beyond current human understanding.

This leads us into deeps of philosophy beyond the scope of these pages, and our preferred means of approach is not by way of philosophising but by the more direct way of systematic training and development of the natural human faculties. Those that provide a personal awareness of the "mind side" of nature.

This does however entail by-passing the concrete mental faculties by an act of faith. Whilst the human intellect may be quite within its rights in seeking for logical proofs before embarking on a journey over unproven ground, the human intellect also has its limitations, and so should not be allowed to rule the roost unchallenged.

It may well be that the intimations from the higher self should be given more weight. These may appear in the form of an "irrational" sense of destiny, or of conscience that something needs to be done, perhaps a quest to be followed, or a particular intuition to follow a new direction.

Thus, says an adage of ancient wisdom "Ask, and it shall be given you; seek and ye shall find; knock, and it shall be opened unto you." So standing outside the door of opportunity and doubting proves nothing but the sterility of lack of faith.

This doorway is in the imagination and leads to the great treasure house of images within. For the most part these are picture images, but there are images in sound as well, and of the more "formless" senses of touch, taste and smell and yet more subtle ones that are not usually included in psychological manuals. Those which are often vehicles of the intuition, as for example when one "senses" the presence of another, even in a darkened room. This sense of presence can manifest also with contacts between the planes of consciousness.

Before we can arrive at the crucial test of finding out the truth of these things for ourselves, we have to develop and train the faculties involved. These faculties are concerned with processing symbolic images and numerous ideas.

Most of the images take their form from experience and perception of forms within the physical world. Some of these forms of everyday life and consciousness may also take on, or be invested with, a significance beyond their own immediate use and purpose. That is, they may serve as reflections of higher modes of expression. That is to say, they may serve as *symbols,* and much of esoteric training consists of learning to identify, to fashion, to interpret, and to channel the higher forces represented by symbols.

Symbols are many and various, the suits and trumps of the Tarot are a common example, and we process them by building them and holding them within the pictorial imagination. They may then become charged with emotional force, and this is to be seen in their application in stories, particularly involving figures of myth and legend. In turn this emotional charging may become the carrier of spiritual energies and intuitive realisations.

In esoteric work symbolic characters and dramas can be formulated deliberately to invoke and harness spiritual forces. In ritual magic this process is simply taken from the pictorial imagination and enacted in a physical environment - of the temple or the lodge. Spiritual realities are thus expressed physically, completing the circuit from spirit to matter and back again.

So much for the role of the pictorial imagination. There is also, however, another major mode of mentation, beyond picture imagery, the realm of ideas and intuitions. These may be expressed in words but not always so.

The practical way to approach this level is by way of meditation, of which there are various forms. That upon which we will concentrate consists of holding the mind steady upon a particular idea, rather than a pictorial image.

To begin with, by the phenomenon known as the association of ideas many related ideas will tend to come into mind. In one form of meditation these can be pursued and meditated upon in their turn, and this is perhaps closest to our usual mode of concentrated thought when we are trying to solve a problem.

The aim of mental meditation of this type is however, not so much to solve mental or physical problems but to bore a hole, so to speak, in the shell of concrete mental ideation to the formless levels beyond. Then intuition may flow in, bringing seemingly irrational but spiritually valid impulses to action or further realisation.

This kind of thing is perhaps most commonly seen when we elect "to sleep" on a problem. The solution, if we are lucky, comes into mind the next morning. This is popularly termed letting "the subconscious" deal with the matter. Although we know very little of what we actually mean by "the subconscious"; it is little more than a convenient label for what we do not understand.

However, in sustained and systematic esoteric training and development, we aim to open up access to this intuitional level at will. This should produce the person who can do the right thing at the right time, largely based upon "hunches" or, at higher levels, a sense of spiritual destiny, even if to the rational mind circumstances seem to advise against this particular mode of action.

What is particularly important about this kind of mentation however, if we refer back to our simple table of faculties, is that we are forming a direct link not only between two levels of the mental plane, but between the higher self and the lower self. In a term borrowed from the east, this is sometimes called the *antaskarana*, or more picturesquely entitled "the rainbow bridge". Other associated imagery is shooting the arrow of spiritual desire from the bow of aspiration, as in William Blake's famous words in his poem *Jerusalem*, or opening up personality consciousness to the world of souls, or form consciousness to the formless worlds.

Chapter 2a

MIND TRAINING
Dion Fortune

In order to appreciate the scope and application of the powers of the trained mind we need to understand the nature of man and his relationship to his environment.

According to popular conceptions, man lives inside his body like a chick inside an egg, and what goes on outside concerns him not at all save in so far as it affects his physical vehicle. That is to say, the physical vehicle alone has any contact with the external universe; consciousness is a closed system except for its relationship with the sense organs it inhabits. This is the basis for the old dictum that nothing is in the mind but what has first been in the senses. A very small amount of unprejudiced observation, however, gives the lie to this. The initiate believes that the mind is related to the world of mind in just the same way as the body is related to the world of matter. Let us study this analogy and see what light it yields us.

The physical body is built up out of a selection of the inorganic substances that constitute the world of matter. This selective discretion appears to be exercised by the tissues composing the body, which have the power to absorb certain substances and ignore others. For instance, if a certain amount of hair from the cow's tail is mixed in with the milk we drink, as it so frequently is, our tissues have the power to absorb the milk and reject the hair, which passes through our bodies unchanged.

The initiate maintains that the mind works in just the same way; that it is built up out of the mind-stuff of the cosmos in exactly the same manner that the physical body is built up out of substances forming the physical universe.

Now it is well known to those who have studied such things that it is only plants that can make direct use of the sunlight in order to work up inorganic mineral substances into organic foodstuffs. No man by sitting in the sun and swallowing soil can do this. All he can do is to eat the plants, or the animals that have already eaten plants. All his food is second-hand.

Now if we apply this analogy to the mind, we should agree with orthodox psychology that nothing can be in the mind that has not come in through the senses; that is to say, all our mental experience must have been assimilated for us by the physical body, which alone, according to this concept, has sense organs. The mind, it is maintained, can no more assimilate mental influences direct than the body can assimilate garden soil; the body with its sense organs doing for the soul of man what the plants do for the animal kingdom.

Now is this true? That is a matter, not of argument but of observation. Has the mind ever been known to assimilate direct? And if so, under what conditions? Direct assimilation of mental influences by the mind is called telepathy, and telepathy is held by recognised authorities to be an established fact. We have, therefore, definite evidence that, under certain conditions, the mind can assimilate what has not been pre-digested for it by the sense organs of the body.

Now this is an exceedingly important point; one might really say that it is one of the pillars of the temple of esoteric philosophy. If the materialistic hypothesis were true, then occult science would be the balderdash the materialist says it is; but the establishment of the fact of telepathy knocks the bottom out of this hypothesis and opens the door to a greatly extended concept of some very important things; in fact it means that we have got to reconsider our whole attitude towards our environment, for we can no longer consider ourselves as closed systems of consciousness, shut up inside our physical bodies, but must reckon upon having direct relations with our mental environment; in varying degrees it is true, but nevertheless quite definitely, even in the most insensitive of us, and in certain cases in a very high degree indeed.

Telepathy is generally understood to be the communication of one person with another by means of thought; a little observation, however, will show us that a much commoner form of communication is the sympathetic induction of moods and emotions. For instance, there are innumerable occasions on record where a friend is seized with an overwhelming sense of dread and depression at the moment when someone meets with disaster. We all know how a depressed or bad tempered person will spread his influence through a house without a word spoken. We also know that certain houses and even certain objects exercise a definite influence, and enquiry usually reveals this influence to be due to the characters of their previous occupants or owners. All these things are so well established that we may safely take them as agreed facts; for though individual instances may be open to question, the actual existence of such phenomena can hardly be questioned by anyone capable of appreciating evidence.

Upon this basis the occultist builds his practical work. He says that mental influence is a fact; but as telepathy has come to mean one particular type of influence, that is to say, the communication of ideas from one mind to another, he reserves the term for that only, and for non-physical influences in general he uses the term psychic, from the Greek word for soul, and then classifies the different types of psychic influence that are known to him, among which telepathy is one.

He classifies these psychic influences into spiritual, mental, astral and magnetic.

Spiritual influence he would declare to be pure life-force, just as the sun gives off pure, uncoloured light. But even as white light contains the potentiality of all colour, so pure spiritual life-force emanating directly from the Creator, contains the potentialities of all the different types of force that build our universe. A spiritual influence consists of an influx of this force upon the spiritual nature of man; but spirit being beyond the immediate apprehension of the human mind, we cannot perceive this influence directly; we only experience it as fullness of life; or, contrarily, if this influence is obstructed, as loss of vitality or loss of general driving force. It is a removal of obstructions and reestablishment of a free flow of spiritual life-force which is the work of psychotherapy.

Mental influence is our old friend telepathy; it is the influence of organised mind upon organised mind as distinguished from the "inorganic" force of pure undifferentiated spirit. The initiate holds, however, that organised minds survive bodily death, which is a concept that greatly extends the sphere of operations, for it means that if telepathy is a fact at all, telepathic communication is possible with the departed; this fact is the corner-stone of spiritualism. It requires only a little imagination, however, to see that it has applications far beyond the field of spiritualism, and might be a factor in both psychopathology and psychotherapy.

With the study of astral influence we open up a very complex and far reaching sphere of investigation. It is upon the astral plane as the esotericist calls this phase of manifestation, that the pure white light of the spiritual life-force gets analysed into its component factors. Upon this plane it is possible for the human mind to perceive it. This is exemplified in the saying that we cannot know God as He is, but can only conceive Him as the sum total of all His qualities; these qualities being the factors which can be distinguished in the spiritual life-force when it operates in the manifested universe.

The whole of the magical technique rests upon this hypothesis, for magic aims at picking up the different types of spiritual force in their pure form and concentrating them. It is to this end that all its technique is directed; and as it is a mental operation, it is performed entirely by the mind, and all the material paraphernalia of ceremonial and symbol are simply to help the mind to concentrate and to exalt the imagination.

Magnetic influence is on the borderline between the mind and matter; it is a form of vitality, probably electric in nature for everything that we know to be true of the functioning of electricity appears to apply to it, but also dependent upon psychic states for its manifestation, using that term in its broadest sense to include both idea and emotion.

These four types of influences are all psychic influences, though their sub-divisions are legion; and we are all capable of both receiving, perceiving, and exerting them, both consciously and unconsciously, in widely varying degrees. Upon one hand is the indifference of the stodgy, unimaginative, self-satisfied and self-centred person, and upon the other are the sensitiveness of the psychic and the powers of the adept. In between is the normal person, who is a good deal more psychic than he realises because he is accustomed to accept the subtle influences by which he is surrounded as a matter of course, and attribute them to the state of his nerves, his stomach, or the weather. What is popularly called "nerves" will invariably be found to contain varying degrees of sensitivity to subtle influences such as we have described. Orthodox medicine can do very little for them because it takes no account of these subtle influences. Unorthodox practitioners, however, often being themselves sensitives, can frequently handle these cases where Harley Street fails.

Having analysed our problem into its component factors, we are now in a position to consider its practical aspects. For all practical purposes it is impossible to differentiate between the mind and the emotions, for all ideas are always emotionally toned in some degree; it is an astro-mental organisation with which we function on the inner planes. This we must bear in view when training.

For the purposes of the mental exercises, however, we simplify our problems as much as possible, and we choose subjects in which there is the largest proportion of mind to the least proportion of emotion; this is one of the reasons why mind-wandering is a problem in the earlier stages, when we are doing the five-finger exercises of the mind that have no emotional associations, for the attention always tends to turn to the most highly emotional aspect of the mental content. However, the power to direct the mind at will is one that is essential to any progress, spiritual or mundane, and the very emptiness of the exercises is part of their value as training material.

We teach the mind to acquire the art of building up and holding steady a mental picture in the imagination. We also teach it to make, and listen to, imaginary speeches. It does not matter what the pictures of speeches are about as long as they are emotionally neutral - anyone can wax eloquent in the imagination upon the subject of grievances, or picture in detail his heart's desire. What is needed is to learn to use the imagination at will, apart from the emotions. This is not as easy as it sounds, but it is the key to a very great deal when we can do it. It means, firstly, that we can direct thought-force at will; and secondly, that the powers that the initiate learns to invoke will never get the upper hand and obsess us so that we lose our mental or moral balance. This is very necessary when we are dealing with astral forces, for they are good servants, but bad masters.

Most schools of occult training, borrowing from one another and following tradition blindly, start their students off by teaching them to visualise a triangle, or a point within a circle, or some such simple object, thinking that the simpler it is, the easier it is. This is a mistake: it is far more difficult to visualise a simple object upon which the attention must be held rigid, as it were, than to visualise an object sufficiently complex for the attention to be able to move from point to point, just as it is easier to balance on a cycle if one is moving at a fair pace than if one is going very slowly. It is better, therefore, to deal at the start with complex subjects, such as a roomful of furniture, or a country walk, because it is so much easier for the mind to achieve attention before it attempts concentration.

The complete stilling of the mind in *samadhi* is a very high degree of concentration indeed, and few Europeans achieve it. Our racial *dharma* being the conquest of matter, however, I doubt whether Europeans find in *samadhi* a profitable goal. I have always believed it to be a great mistake to try to disincarnate while still in the flesh. It is a kind of spiritual suicide, and in my experience it brings pathology rather than blessing. All we need aim at in our method of training is adequate concentration, and to employ certain technical devices to aid us, such as symbolism and ritual.

The power having been achieved to create clear-cut mental pictures at will, and to hold them for as long as is desired, we are now ready for the next step, which is to take one of these neutral, emotionless pictures and fill it with force drawn from spiritual sources. This we do by choosing some object that shall symbolically represent the force we wish to draw to us, and while picturing it clearly in the mind's eye, work up in ourselves a feeling corresponding to the force we wish to contact in its cosmic form. For instance, we make ourselves feel compassionate if we want to attract a healing force. We then picture in our imagination the cosmic force in a ray of appropriately coloured light descending upon our chosen symbol. If we do this clearly, and are working along the line of cosmic law and not constructing chimeras that have no possibility of life in them, we shall feel a tremendous influx of power of the chosen type, and the symbol we have built and ensouled will only have to be visualised in future for us to pick up these contacts again very readily.

That is the true occult technique. It may be said that I am giving away the secrets of practical occultism in thus explaining it; but these secrets can no more be given away than can the secrets of practical violin playing, for to use this method presupposes a trained mind and a thorough knowledge of cosmic law; these are things that have to be worked for.

Chapter 2b

MIND TRAINING
Gareth Knight

Techniques of training the mind usually concern themselves with the control of the imagery that is present in the conscious mind of the everyday personality. Ultimately, however, mind training extends all the way from spiritual and intuitive contacts with the higher mind through to control of the autonomic nervous system and muscular consciousness of the physical body.

This of course is a vast field, and the type of training will depend upon what form of esoteric development is being sought. In the East disciples of yoga spend a very great deal of time and effort in arousing and directing etheric forces within the aura. This calls for specific and quite difficult physical postures, allied to complex breathing techniques, accompanied by specific visualisations to affect the directions of subtle force flow. Sustained work upon these lines over a matter of years can bring about startling results in control of the physical vehicle - including suspended animation, bi-location and levitation, attributes only associated with rare sanctity in the west, and then involuntarily.

The performance of spectacular tricks is not of course the principal aim of such disciplines. They are however an outer sign of the considerable inner feats of control of consciousness allied to the union of the higher vehicles of consciousness with the lower. Yoga indeed means "union".

However, to attain such a degree of control calls for a rigorously dedicated monastic life style, one that is not open to the average esoteric student in the west. Although certain elementary exercises based upon yoga training can be salutary, as a branch of health and beauty regimes, the main thrust of advanced training in the west follows a different route.

The first objective is to exercise some kind of discipline and control over the moving talking picture screen of our stream of consciousness, our own personal "virtual reality" device, that sometimes obsessively runs off its own loops of fantasy, driven by various emotions and channelled by pet ideas.

We can begin to bring some control and order into this by simple daily exercises, either by striving to make the mind a blank, or by holding it still, within a narrow focus, upon some particular object or idea.

Making the mind a blank is no easy feat, and is of no great use in itself. The only use for a blank mind is to allow something worthwhile to come along and fill it and if this is of the higher intuitions or impulsions of the spirit then that is all to the good. There is a fairly well trodden mystical way known as the *via negativa*, or negative way, whereby the mystic seeks to find a way to God without the use of images - on the grounds that no image in itself can be anything else but a veil before the real - and that one needs to get beyond created forms to reach the uncreate reality behind them all.

The training of most esoteric students of the west, and particularly for those who aspire to techniques of ritual, is however by the *via positiva*, or positive way. That is to say, by the use and help of images.

We can start by concentrating upon some particular idea or phrase, perhaps of a general aspirational nature. Dion Fortune quotes Coué's famous phrase, particularly popular when the New Thought movement was in its hey day "Every day and in every way I am getting better and better". There is perhaps something rather brash - even commercial sounding about this. It is not very far from the kind of psychological training that one finds in certain schools of salesmanship. Some nuns, it is said, attracted to Coué's methods preferred to insert a devout corollary "Every day and in every way, *by the will of God*, I am getting better and better." However, it would have been just as appropriate, perhaps, for them to have gone back to their rosaries, where - in the devotional ambience of a long sequence of Paternosters and Ave Marias - the same psychological principles apply.

However, as far as the training of the ritual magician is concerned, the purpose of the exercise is not one of devotional religious practice nor of psychological confidence boosting. It is simply a system of mental exercises, the equivalent of the muscular exercises we might undertake in order to keep physically fit.

Just as different physical exercises will benefit different parts of the body, so concentrating upon different types of subject will develop different parts of the soul and mind. We have, in our last chapter, divided consciousness into various levels; into spiritual, moral, intuitional, rational, visionary, emotive, and physical/ etheric. Different means of mind working apply to each.

In practical terms we probably do best to start more or less in the middle of this psychological spectrum, with the emotionally and morally neutral concrete mind. The words or images we use are of no great consequence to begin with. We are primarily concerned with establishing a discipline.

This is a matter of forming habit and custom patterns. Of setting aside a certain period each day to the practice of meditation, and not deviating from it. The period set aside need not be long, ten or fifteen minutes is ample, until the practice is well established over a number of months, once or perhaps twice a day. Long periods devoted to the exercise between irregular gaps are no substitute or compensation for the regular performance of the minimum requirement.

When one has been performing this kind of practice for some time, its value will have become so apparent that no more discipline is needed than applies to sitting down to lunch, and the inner perceptions will have attained a state of atunement throughout much of waking life. Not indiscriminately open to all the psychic winds that blow, but poised on permanent stand-by.

Sentences culled from an esoteric text that personally appeals can provide plenty of material for meditation of this type. Thus, turning for example to the first few paragraphs of Dion Fortune's *Mystical Qabalah* we might select sentences of the order of:

> "the fountain whence our tradition springs"
> "the Yoga of the West"
> "the mysticism of Israel".

Each of these short phrases contain the potential for very considerable expansion, according to our own conscious or unconscious knowledge, so keeping a diary in which to make notes of any "realisations" is one of the first disciplines of the western aspirant. According to tradition, it is possible to tap into a pool of ancient knowledge by these means, and if this is the case then the student may eventually develop into a teacher or writer upon esoteric subjects.

However, this advanced application is not the aim of the exercise as far as the beginner is concerned. Indeed, for those who already have a degree of natural psychism, this type of exercise may well seem to close it down. This is all to the good, for when this mental discipline has been observed, keeping the mind focused about a specific constellation of words or ideas, then a more precise and reliable psychism can be developed.

The next stage is to spend the time of meditation, not upon a phrase or sentence, but upon a pictorial image, and of these there are various kinds.

There is a very abstract form of imagery such as may be found, for example, in Dion Fortune's "received" communication *The Cosmic Doctrine*, in which the communicator quite categorically states that "these images are designed to train the mind, not inform it." In other words, it is not a question of filling the concrete mind with verbal concepts but of developing a direct contact with the intuitional levels of the higher self, or soul consciousness.

The type of imagery is of the order of a point in space beginning to move, and then because of dual forces within its nature, taking on a curved path which eventually leads to the formation of a great ring. This great ring then sets up a series of secondary currents and movements that form another ring at right angles to itself. And then through the interaction of the two rings so formed, the inner one begins to spin, and so forms a sphere, within which a complex pattern of rings and rays and vortices are born, forming the seven planes of a universe, its twelve types of expression, and the myriad stars and divine sparks that go to form the created universe.

There are plenty of other sources for this type of imagery it should be said, and not all as rigorously abstract. Some of the famous Rosicrucian diagrams associated with Robert Fludd, for instance, may serve as well to provide imagery of this nature. Or from medieval times the patterns of the heavens as depicted in Dante's *Paradiso*.

Sustained meditation on this type of imagery will open up access to higher levels of consciousness, or in other words, "tune" the focus of consciousness to required inner levels for magic to work. But the lower levels are equally important, if we seek to develop a balanced practitioner.

For the lower levels we still seek a mode of consciousness that resonates with spiritual realities and this is best revealed in the realms of symbolism, and any system of legend or mythology will prove a rich source of material. Of particular value in this respect are the Arthurian legends, as they have a complete run through from the ancient depths of racial memory represented by the Cauldron of Ceridwen, or the Round Table of Merlin and Guinevere, and the realms of the Ladies of the Lake, right on through aspects of medieval chivalry and heroic and courtly aspirations of a gradually civilising society, to the mystical heights of the Holy Graal. In *The Secret Tradition in Arthurian Legend* which is based upon pioneering work by Dion Fortune and those who followed her along these lines, I have endeavoured to map out a tentative structure of esoteric training and mystery working.

Another rich source of symbolic material may be found in the Tarot, which like the stellar symbolism found in astrology, is often sadly abused and reduced to popular fortune telling. But at root the Tarot is a self contained structure of related symbolism, from the four-fold symbolism of the suits, with their basic sign, number and court card effigies through to the twenty-two trump cards each of which is a compendium of archetypal symbolism in itself. It is possible to train oneself very adequately in the mysteries simply by fashioning in meditation one's own set of Tarot designs. I have described various ritual and divinatory applications in *Tarot & Magic* (formerly *'The Treasure House of Images'*) and *The Magical World of the Tarot*.

There is also a vast collection of symbolism to be found laid out in related function and pattern in the Tree of Life of the Qabalah, details of which may be found in Dion Fortune's *Mystical Qabalah* upon which I myself was first trained, and my own *A Practical Guide to Qabalistic Symbolism* which in its turn leans heavily on what I first learned in the school which Dion Fortune founded.

However, apart from these compendia of esoteric symbolism, there is another line of training which strikes directly at the facility of handling internal imagery. This is simply to construct one's own scenes in the imagination. To begin with, some actual location within the store of personal memory can be very helpful, such as taking the dog for a walk in your imagination through once familiar scenes, possibly of childhood.

From this it is a short step to go upon completely imaginary journeys, at first in naturalistic settings, prosaic inner circumstances, but then gradually developing towards symbolic landscapes and meetings with various imagined beings. In one sense this is very close to the imaginative working of a novelist, playwright or short story writer - and indeed in these esoteric exercises lie considerable aids to development of the powers of self expression and the creative imagination.

Moving into deeper esoteric waters, we may then embark upon completely symbolic journeys, of which the traditional "paths" between the different spheres on the Tree of Life are an excellent start. We may commence at one sphere on the Tree of Life, imagining it as a kind of temple or structure dedicated to the relevant planetary symbolism, and making our way to the next sphere, also visualised as a building or site of some kind. On the way we progress through three types of symbol - first the Tarot card which is allocated to the path, seen as a kind of picture veil at its beginning, through which we may pass. Then arriving a some kind of sacred grove or symbolic mid-point marked by the appropriate Hebrew letter. And towards the end of the path coming under the influence in some pictorial way of the astrological sign.

There is a set system of correspondences which may be used, although such systems may vary. French Qabalism for instance, deriving from Eliphas Levi and "Papus" has a different system of attributions from those used in the English speaking world, which derive from the Hermetic Order of the Golden Dawn. Yet both systems work reasonably well for experienced occultists who work with them.

From this it follows that one has no need to stick slavishly to any one particular system of traditional correspondences as one gains confidence and experience. The inner worlds are capable of infinite expansion, but because of this, it is perhaps wise for those who are finding their way within it for the first time to structure their efforts within an accepted and stable symbol structure. To learn to walk round the walled garden without trampling the flower beds or falling into the lily pond, before venturing out into the wider fields of the unseen, where there may be deeper and murkier swamps and ditches awaiting the unwary traveller.

Again, these are exercises within the imagination, in full control of consciousness. Awareness of the physical environment may well fall into abeyance in the course of any such exercise, but the practice of ritual magic, by its very nature, is not one that seeks passive trance states, or abandoning the physical body in some kind of projection. Still less does it condone the use of illegal substances as a short cut to seeking altered states of consciousness.

It is a means of conscious action upon the physical plane, enacting spiritual principles in symbolic terms, whilst holding awareness open to inner and outer planes simultaneously. It is this dual function of consciousness whilst in full control of the physical vehicle that is the aim of the exercises that have been described.

Chapter 3a

THE USE OF RITUAL
Dion Fortune

To many people, the use of a set formula in the work of spiritual unfolding and attainment appears incongruous and distasteful. There is a deep-rooted prejudice against "vain observances", which is not without foundation and justification, for in so many cases the observance had taken the place of the unfolding. Unless there is understanding of the rites as a means to an end, and a sound grasp of their rationale, their observance soon degenerates into superstition and waste of time, neither pleasing to God nor beneficial to man. When, however, the rationale of ritual is understood it is never permitted to degenerate into superstition, but is employed as it is meant to be employed, as a technical method in the psychology of super-consciousness.

Ritual is of value simply and solely for its effect on the consciousness of the participants. I have never seen any evidence adduced to support the hypothesis that ritual is efficacious apart from the mental work put into it. For instance, a gramophone record of a ritual, left to play by itself in an empty room, would produce no results, astral or otherwise. Equally, a ritual done without understanding produces as little power as water boiling in an open vessel. Witness the Lord's Supper as celebrated in a Nonconformist congregation. To obtain any results with ritual, either as celebrant or participant, you must know what you are about; in order to arrive at this understanding, let us analyse the factors that go to the making of a ritual, and observe that these hold good for all types of ritual.

First and foremost, there is the psychological effect, the exaltation of consciousness of the participants. Secondly, by means of the exalted consciousness, contacts are made with spiritual forces. Thirdly, the means used to make these contacts are what, in the technical language of occultism, are called thought-forms. These three factors are present in any rite, however simple, or however elaborate.

From the point of view of practical mind training, the aspect we are most interested in is the exaltation of consciousness; and in the light of what we have already learnt in these pages, its modus operandi is easily understood. Coué has already formulated its law for us. The deeper levels of the mind can be influenced by profound feeling and prolonged attention. He strove to find a substitute for spontaneous emotion because he knew of no way of producing it at will, and he found his substitute in prolonged attention produced by means of a kind of litany recited with the aid of an undenominational rosary of knotted string.

By means of ritual we are able to take advantage of both these methods of subconscious appeal, the one powerfully reinforcing the other. By means of the performance of a set rite we obtain prolonged attention, and by means of the use of "conditioned symbols" to make up the rite, we generate emotion. By means of a mood, or emotionally toned state of mind, we are able to get into touch with the corresponding spiritual force, and by means of a rite we are able to induce a mood. That, briefly, is the rationale of ceremonial as understood by the initiate and as used by him.

To say this, however, is not to claim that exalted states of consciousness can only be obtained by the use of set ceremonies. They can be, and frequently are, achieved spontaneously by sheer devotion; but this cannot be commanded, and there are many deep and dark nights of the soul for those who depend on faith alone for the achievement of these higher states of consciousness. It would also be true to say that the higher aspects of these states can only be achieved by pure devotion. But by availing ourselves of the technique of religious psychology we can free consciousness from its self-imposed limits and lend it wings for its flight.

It is well known in physiology that minute daily quantities of vitamins are essential to health; very little is needed, but that little is indispensable. And so it is with the soul; there is a minimum of spiritual experience without which the soul cannot keep its poise; by means of ceremonial we are able to ensure it at least that minimum.

And how is this achieved? Once again by the use of that all-important factor, the imagination. The attention is held, the imagination is directed, a mood is achieved, the spiritual exaltation follows automatically.

The rules which govern the design of a ritual are the rules which govern the holding of attention. First and foremost, there is the emotionally charged idea and the symbol that represents it, whether it be a symbol to which we respond spontaneously or whether we have been "conditioned" to it. Then there is the appeal of sound through pitch and rhythm, an appeal which stirs the very foundations of our being. There is also the appeal of incense, which is a primordial appeal. Then there are the conditions under which a rite is performed. These should be such as lull the mind and render it receptive, therefore the effect of a ritual is most potent when it is performed in a dim light with all other sounds excluded, so that there is nothing to distract the attention. Finally, there is the well-known effect of reiteration.

These, you will say, are the conditions that the hypnotist uses to get his victim "under". Certainly they are: and he uses them because he knows they are effectual. But when these conditions are applied in ritual, the human mind of the hypnotist is absent, and its place is taken by the Holy Spirit. By these simple devices the lower mind is manipulated so that the higher mind may come into action.

In using such methods, however, one needs to know what one is about; I am far from denying, in fact I wish to point out unequivocally, that in ignorant or unscrupulous hands the effects obtained by ritual lend themselves to abuse. But as I have so often said before in connection with the practical application of the occult knowledge, a medicine that is potent enough to produce good effects in the right dose, will be potent enough to produce poisonous effects in an overdose, or if used when contra-indicated. The drug that is harmless to the patient in any dose is apt also to be harmless to the disease in every dose. A very objectionable ascendancy can be obtained over people by the clever use of impressive rituals, even by charlatans, and it has been not infrequently done, to my certain knowledge.

What guarantee, then, has a student who enters an esoteric school that this power will not be abused?

His guarantee should be found in his early training. Anyone who has had his mind trained as I have indicated is unhypnotisable. The reason for this will readily be seen. First, we have concentration; secondly, we have the power to turn from one object of concentration to another at will. Now hypnotism depends upon the power to obsess the concentration by a given object, like a hen with its beak held to a line of chalk on the floor. If a person has the power to change over from one object of concentration to another at will, you cannot obsess his attention. He merely changes over, and the would-be hypnotist is "done". An interesting example of this is recorded in Kipling's well-known novel of the Indian secret service, *Kim*, wherein the boy, being tested for suggestibility, resists the hypnotic influence by reciting the multiplication table.

The initiate therefore, who desires to obtain his results in the speediest and most effectual manner, and at the same time to have them completely under control all the time, makes great use of formulae, beginning and ending all operations with them, even the simple operation of meditation. By this means he raises consciousness quickly and certainly from "cold"; and, what is even more important, returns it at will to normal when the operation is finished; to fail to do this is to invite nerve trouble, for no one in an exalted state of consciousness is in a fit condition to cope with the rubs and stresses of daily life.

Now, you will ask, what kind of formulae does he use? He simply applies to his Inner Group knowledge the methods he has been taught in the Outer Court. The initiate imagines himself to be clad in the robes of his grade and seated in a symbolic representation of a sanctuary which he has been taught how to formulate. The person who has done that has very little trouble with mind wandering. Students may think the picturing of a room in the imagination is a trivial performance, but it leads on to the picturing of the symbolic temples with all their elaborate detail of symbolism when the advanced knowledge is available, and if you cannot picture your familiar bedroom with detail and clarity, and hold it stead for the few minutes of the meditation, how are you going to picture the elaborate composite symbols and obtain the results they are capable of giving?

Having cut himself off from all extraneous influences by means of the "composition of place" as St. Ignatius, who was the first to teach it outside the Mysteries, called it, the student next picks up the contact of his tradition by means of the formula that is given him, and these contacting formulae are the things that are kept really secret in the Mysteries, and are never committed to paper; and as they consist as much of knowing how to do, as well as knowing what to do, they can no more be betrayed than the secrets of Kreisler's violin technique. Consequently there is no legitimate reason for making a mystery of them, and it is much more interesting for students, and they will work much more effectually, if they know the reason for the things they are made to do, and the purposes to which they will ultimately be applied. It also shows them why it is useless for a student to "fake" his meditation record, for as soon as he is given the actual occult work to do, his fake is revealed, for he cannot do it. He is wasting nobody's time but his own if he does the meditations carelessly, or according to some other method that he considers preferable. If, instead of the clear-cut visualisation, he slides off into day-dreaming in his meditation, when he is given the actual symbols to work with, he will also slide off into day-dreaming without being able to help himself, and the symbols will not work for him. Meditation training can no more be faked than learning to ride a bicycle. If you have practised so little that you have not attained a steady balance, no filling in of forms will prevent you from falling off when you get among the trains and the traffic. These things adjust themselves automatically even in the correspondence courses, because magic is a practical system and proves itself by results. If you have not mastered your technique in the Outer, you will not obtain results in the Inner.

Chapter 3b

THE USE OF RITUAL
Gareth Knight

Magical ritual is a technique for raising consciousness that has close affiliations with theatre. Indeed theatre first grew out of religious festivals in ancient Greece, in festivals of Dionysos where a priest taking the part of the god chanted a litany with responses from a chorus.

From a litany based upon a story of the god there developed the action of first two and then three or more protagonists. This was still very much in a hieratic form of presentation, with the actors wearing stylised masks and elevated in height upon raised boots. From these religious festivals and their later development we inherit the great dramatic tragedies of Aeschylus, Sophocles, Euripides, drawing upon legendary stories of gods and heroes. The purpose of these dramas was a religious and moral one: to "purge the soul" by the evocation of terror and pity.

Magical ritual, it should be said, does not aim to "purge the souls" of its celebrants with pity and terror in the ancient Greek sense. Nonetheless it is a means whereby the soul may be very deeply stirred, and this because drama, even when indifferently performed, is a very powerful technique, and even more so when the subject of the drama is of a symbolic, mythopoeic or religious character.

Much of the powerful effect of drama comes from being a live interaction between performer and audience. A film does not have quite the same impact even with the presence of an audience, and there is also a noticeable difference between a film seen in a crowded cinema and one seen on television by a solitary viewer. Much the same applies in the more rough and ready drama of a sporting contest - however interesting it may be to the home television viewer, there is no real substitute for the thrill of actual presence as part of the crowd, who in their way are actually participating with the contestants.

Thus, what Coleridge called the "willing suspension of disbelief" that occurs when we watch a company of actors performing on a stage before us, can have a profound effect upon our emotions and affect us for some considerable time after. This effect may be enhanced with the addition of music, whether in popular show or grand opera, and it is worth noting that film, because it is a mechanical medium, finds it essential to have supporting music in order to gain the emotional impact that it otherwise lacks.

These theatrical dynamics are therefore what we seek to harness for the purpose of esoteric training in ritual magic, with the possible addition of olfactory stimulation by the use of incense. Regular performance of magical ritual can have a much more rapid and profound effect upon the inner vehicles of the esoteric student than individual meditation.

The main difference between magic and the theatre lies in the subject matter and intention. Magic is not seeking to entertain a passive audience, and its subject matter is directly concerned with the portrayal and representation of inner realities. Thus all the "props" of a magical temple will have a symbolic meaning and value, with the intention of producing a deep effect upon the souls of those participating.

The technique of a ritual officer is also different from the technique of an actor. A trained actor who is "putting on a performance" by means of skilled dramatic technique may be completely "dead" as regards magical function if he is placing an ego blockage in what should be a free flowing channel between inner and outer levels. In ceremonial magic, although skills in voice production and physical movement have their place, the prime requirement is sincerity; a sincerity that stems from a dedication to what one is doing and a faith in its reality.

The general tradition and practice in Western esoteric circles is for the student to learn the techniques by participating in magical rituals. First as a member of the group without any outwardly active part, and later, as confidence and skill develops, being entrusted with various ceremonial functions. Eventually to act as magus of a rite, and to write and perform original rituals.

All who attend a magical ritual are participants, whether they realise it or not, for it is the pooled consciousness of those present that makes for the atmosphere and provides much of the power. Anyone sitting in simply as a spectator will not only fail to see anything of much value or entertainment, but will be a positive dead weight on the efforts of all others present. Hence the need for vetting membership and the comparative rarity of publicly performed rituals.

Thus it is the duty of every member of a group to visualise vividly all the imagery that is described. For it is not only the outward show that matters. The symbols that are present in the physical lodge, be they part of the general furniture, such as altar, pillars, lights, or more specific symbolic items such as swords, wands or chalices, are principally there to act as a focus of attention. They are not necessarily noumenous objects in themselves.

And when we speak of a focus of attention for all present, we do not confine our remarks to those who are simply *physically* present but to all who are *psychically* present. This may include those who are no longer blessed or encumbered with physical bodies, and in a magical working inner membership is just as exclusively controlled as outer membership, and for much the same reasons. Powerful imaginative work is being undertaken that requires the undivided attention of those who are sufficiently skilled, dedicated and trusted to tune to higher and more potent levels of consciousness.

To those of the outer world such aims may seem to range from the harmless and deluded to the sinister and dangerous, but to the dedicated and trained ritual magician it is all very real and very worthwhile. Ritual magic is, by its very nature, a specialisation, but someone has to do it. Indeed throughout the ages it seems likely that someone always has done it, sometimes at risk of religious persecution, but in modern secular times generally only at risk of ridicule - totalitarian regimes and religious bigots of various kinds excepted.

Just as theatre is one form of art amongst many, so is ritual magic one form of esoteric technique amongst many. It follows that just as any of the arts can be the medium for a whole range of human experience from the banal, even the degraded, to the sublime, so magical ritual will reflect the moral integrity and spiritual motivation of its practitioners.

Yet insofar that magical ritual is generally part and parcel of a means of spiritual development, wherein high ethical standards are expected and demanded of its practitioners, there is little substance in the more lurid speculations that inflame the imaginations of readers of popular occult fiction. It may be helpful therefore, if we briefly describe the type of ritual that might be performed by an active magical group working within the Western Mystery Tradition by citing an actual example.

In this instance, the initiative came from an inner plane contact who had strong affiliations with the 1st World War, and the group was requested to build up upon the astral plane, by means of the pooled and directed imagination of all present, and accompanied by physical ritual actions, a series of chapels dedicated to the victims of war. That which follows, although initially performed as part of a ritual, is equally suitable as a meditation for individual performance.

In the first chapel, which is a construct behind the war memorial of a cathedral or similar place of worship, a rectangular room of modest size is seen, the lighting low, the walls of rough stone, with a plain and bare altar, and behind this a tabernacle draped with purple cloth. All is faded and dull. Upon the ceiling a vast rose cross spreading its arms to the four quarters, the rose at its centre, larger and more perfect than any earthly rose, and a deep red in colour.

Below, on either side of the central aisle, are figures of people praying - dark, hunched, penitent figures. The souls of victims of conscience. Victims who rarely find their way into the prayers of others, namely the soldiers who did the killing in wars. In our time it is difficult to imagine the sense of duty and obligation that forced ordinary men to kill one another against the inclinations of their own nature. One, who won the Military Cross in the 1st World War, described himself as "a conscientious objector with a very seared conscience" and there were many thousands of others. Many believed that they were damned, that their actions for king and country had stained their souls irredeemably, and in the after death condition, turned away in shame and guilt from the Light of Christ. In more recent times, among the living, veterans of wars like Vietnam have also suffered cruelly in this way.

The ritual duty of all present at this working is to bring the light and mercy of Christ into this chapel for the redemption of these souls, damned only by their own consciences. To feel an immense wave of love and compassion for the dark souls on each side of the aisle, while you place a small personal token upon the altar. As you do so, the purple drape is pulled off the tabernacle; underneath it is golden and shining, as if reflecting light from an unseen sun. Then its doors are flung open and a great golden light shines out from within, illuminating the whole chapel. At this, the rose upon the rose cross above begins to shed its petals, slowly at first, but gradually increasing until the air was filled with them, and as they fall changing from blood red to pure brilliant white. And no matter how many are shed the rose remains intact, and the whole chapel is filled with golden light and white petals, bringing comfort and forgiveness to all in need of it.

In the next chapel, above the first by a spiral stair, and of like proportions, a plethora of red votive lights are to be seen all around, fixed to the walls, hanging from the ceiling and placed on every available surface, flickering softly. Once again there are souls kneeling in prayer in the pews on either side, dimly seen in the soft light. These are the unstained victims of war, those who have suffered through circumstance or misfortune. The wives, mothers, sweethearts, friends and relatives of the soldiers. Civilians who lost their lives without ever taking an active part in the fighting. Soldiers whose consciences, for whatever reason, are not bloodied, but who have been killed in action. Those who have watched their friends and colleagues die and have been powerless to intervene. The doctors and nurses and other non-combatants who risked - and perhaps lost - their lives in trying to help others. All united by sacrifice, whether willing or not.

The altar, as before, plain and bare, has behind it, high up on the wall, a framed photograph of a young soldier of the 1st World War, smiling and carrying a walking stick. This picture is somehow alive and interactive, for it is of the one who mediated this particular ritual. Underneath is a large representation of the Sacred Heart, surmounted by an equal armed cross, and all surrounded by a ring of thorns. It is of bright gold, but in the soft light the metal appears dark.

Again, as you place a small token upon this altar, the golden heart begins to swell with light, until the crown of thorns becomes a great glowing circle, like the sun, and the heart within it can be seen shining with a rich purple-red light. The brightness of this is almost too great to behold, but we are aware that it is also starting to beat, and with every pulse of the great heart the golden light streams out from it in waves until the whole chapel is filled with light, a symbol of ultimate sacrifice beating out streams of light and compassion for all these souls who have themselves made sacrifices, many of which may have been devastating on a personal level, and the comfort that this light will bring them is charged into the atmosphere, for the rewards they will receive are great.

In the third chapel, which is upon the topmost level, it is difficult to see very much as the whole chapel seems filled with a greyish mist, accompanied by an atmosphere of antiquity, but in an abstract, non-specific sense.

Here we may find any number of souls praying in the pews and from all kinds of age, nationality and background, because this chapel is for the use of all souls with any connection with war and anyone may come and pray here. But in the gloom it is difficult to distinguish individuals, and no features are visible, just vague shapes. Everything is more abstract than in the other chapels, because this is not the domain of individuals but of group consciousness, and "spirit of place". Certain places on earth seem to be centres of war and conflict throughout history - places such as Ypres, Sarajevo, Jerusalem and much of Ireland to name but a few examples. The thick grey mist which is virtually choking the air in this chapel is the manifestation of this warlike impulse, the cloud that obscures the good intentions of men, the blind, hazy atmosphere which prevails in those places on earth where war is a frequent and bloody occurrence, the dark clouding over of reason in the group consciousness which provokes whole groups of people to savagery and violence.

As you make your way toward the altar you are able to make out a shadowy cloaked figure behind it, which seems to be a man holding aloft a lantern, but the mist is too thick to see properly. As you place your final token upon this altar the figure with the lantern moves forward and the lantern begins to glow brightly, cutting through the mist. You realise that it is the figure of Christ himself, and as he comes forward his hood is pushed aside to reveal his face, and light begins to emanate from him until even the lantern seems dim by comparison. All around the mist shrinks back and dissipates into nothing and in a few moments the chapel is clear and bright and filled with inestimable light. Gradually the walls of the chapel fade out of sight and you are standing in the open in the middle of a vast field of poppies which are gently swaying in a summer breeze. Above in the eastern sky is the form of a rose cross with the sacred heart at its centre, streaming out light and peace.

In many respects, this type of ritual might be seen as a type of intercessory prayer, for many souls, living or dead, still in torment or in conflict. It differs from intercessory prayer however by being a detailed and deliberate construct.

In ritual performance its magical dynamics were provided by actual representations of the tabernacle, the sacred heart, the lantern, being placed upon the physical altar within the lodge, along with poppies and representatives of the tools of war - a bayonet, and bullets, together with an apple, which as a preliminary part of the ritual were passed from hand to hand of all present to the accompaniment of the lines of *Arms and the Boy* by the war poet Wilfred Owen, who was seen as a kind of guide or introductor to the chapels.

> Let the boy try along this bayonet-blade
> How cold steel is, and keen with hunger of blood;
> Blue with all malice, like a madman's flash;
> And thinly drawn with famishing for flesh.
>
> Lend him to stroke these blind, blunt bullet-leads
> Which long to nuzzle in the hearts of lads,
> Or give him cartridges of fine zinc teeth,
> Sharp with the sharpness of grief and death.
>
> For his teeth seem for laughing round an apple.
> There lurk no claws behind his fingers supple;
> And God will grow no talons at his heels,
> Nor antlers through the thickness of his curls.

These words served in effect as what is technically known as a "composition of mood" - a device to induce all present into thinking and feeling the same way as a preparation for what is to follow. And indeed, in this instance, not so far distant from the "pity and terror" that was the aim of Greek religious dramaturgy, but raised by spiritual intention into intercession and compassion. And the actual handling of the symbolic artefacts in this highly charged context brought a degree of reality and realisation that is one of the aims of a properly conducted ritual.

Chapter 4a

PSYCHIC PERCEPTION
Dion Fortune

We have spoken hitherto of the positive, constructive work that is done by a trained mind in the Mystery working; we now come to the reverse of the coin, and will consider the passive, perceptive powers of such a mind, for it is of little use to construct thought-forms to aid you in your work if you are insensible to the influences of the forms so constructed. We have already had something to say on the subject of telepathy, and the reader is asked to bear this in mind, for it concerns the first principles of what we are about to consider in its practical application.

Psychism (as distinguished from intuitional awareness of spiritual forces) may be defined as the technique of the perception of thought-forms, just as magic is the technique of their making and employment. In psychism, which is a formal mode of consciousness in contrast to the formless consciousness of intuition, it is the subconscious mode of mentation that predominates. For opening up the subconscious content, there are two modes of procedure available to us. One is the method employed in the ancient Mysteries whereby an appeal is made to the imagination by means of symbols. These set up reactions and deliver the subconscious content on the surface in symbolic form, which whether interpreted or not, produces its effects. The other method is that of psycho-analysis, associated with the names of Freud and Jung. It likewise delivers the subconscious contents on the surface in symbolic form, but it then sets to work to interpret them by means of a dogma that takes no account of anything outside of subconsciousness itself.

But one cannot interpret the specialised anatomical structure of any creature except in relation to the conditions to which it is adapted, and it appears to me that psychology would be wise to learn from the senior science of biology in this matter and see what will be yielded in practical therapeutic results if the soul of man is interpreted in terms of its end as well as of the instinctive means to that end.

The methods of the ancient Mysteries, being far removed from modern thought, only yield results to the non-thinker, and are inhibited to the thinker. The methods of the psychotherapists, being far removed from the nature of the soul itself, are singularly barren of results in comparison to the amount of tillage that is given to the ground. Could we, however, combine the two, it is probable that we should have something that would accommodate itself to the nature of the soul, and at the same time prove acceptable to the modern mentality. Let us then approach psychism by the psychoanalytical route and see what results we obtain.

Let us take as the basis of our hypothesis the concept that the mind can respond to purely mental influences. There is so much evidence in support of this that it can hardly be denied, and many scientists of standing have declared themselves satisfied with the evidence and prepared to accept telepathy as an established fact, whatever may be said for the credentials of a given case.

Let us concede, then, that there is in the mind something analogous to the eye. This may seem pretty crude to anyone whose mind is habituated to accurate thinking, but it need not be so very crude if approached from the right angle. The eye, we are told, had a rudimentary beginning in the history of evolution; and in such simple creatures as keep up the old tradition, reaction to light is spread over the whole body surface, minute as that may be, and it is not until we have progressed some way in the path of evolving life that we get the concentrated spot of pigment which ultimately becomes the eye. Might we not conceive, then, that a certain degree of capacity to react to mental influences is spread all over the mind of average folk, but that in some it might be concentrated into the psychological analogy of a pigment spot, and that the method of the Mysteries can build up such a pigment spot of highly coloured images in relation to any given subject?

Let us borrow another point from psychology. A complex is defined as an organised constellation of ideas with a definite emotional tone. An organised system of ideas will naturally be much less susceptible to the impact of subtle influences than unattached individual ideas which might be conceived of as sliding freely over one another, like the molecules in a liquid. We should expect to find then, that two types of person would prove to be more susceptible to psychic influences than the rest of us - those who have no organised systems of ideas, that is to say, the ignorant; and those who have no emotional bias, that is to say, those who are free from the bondage of desire; and this is what we do actually find upon observation.

Leaving aside the ignorant, who furnish us with our primitive, untrained psychics, which do not interest us in this connection, let us consider the mentality of the man who is free from desire. Obviously he is a man of the highest spiritual attainments. So high that it is difficult for the average man to conceive his viewpoint at all. Is there, then, for the rank and file of life's march, any intermediate stage between blank emptiness of intellectual content and this lofty achievement? Yes, there is, and it is obtained by a technique. The results, considered as phenomena, will not equal the results obtained by either the saint or the savage, but they will take us no inconsiderable way upon our journey, and will give us that gift not lightly to be esteemed - a sense of certainty concerning things invisible.

We shall get much light upon this technique if we consider the mechanism of the dream as demonstrated by Freud. He showed clearly that the images in a given dream could be traced to influences operating within the mind itself, which picked up the images lying among the contents of the chambers of memory, and built them up into a living picture which represented the subconscious motives and feelings as clearly as a political cartoon represents the views of its designer. As ideas are woven into complexes, it followed that for every one idea appearing in the cartoon, there were hundreds, or even thousands of associated ideas that would trail after it into consciousness when evoked by analysis. It is this *embarras de richesse* that creates the problems of psychoanalysis of the classic school. If, as the Preacher said, of the making of books there is no end, and if each book is of the nature of James Joyce's *Ulysses*, the problem is rendered insoluble by its very complexity if we approach it in an attitude of pure detachment and observation. Some principle of selection we must have if the matter is to come within the range of practical politics.

It is not for me to teach the psychologists their business, however great the need, therefore let us go on to consider the analogy between the dream as known to the Freudian and the vision as known to the psychic. It is obvious that they are blood relations. The Freudian declares, and up to a certain point I think he is right, that it is the emotion which is in the mind that selects the images that appear in the dream. Let us conclude then that there is some selective influence at work determining the images that are built up into the closely similar cartoon of the vision. Might this influence be the dynamism of thought itself? I see no reason to repudiate this idea, and if it were true, it would explain many things otherwise baffling. Let us therefore take it as a working hypothesis and see where it leads us.

Supposing a person is sitting in a lodge that is working a ceremonial ritual, and he makes his mind a blank and observes the images that arise therein, he will find, as one by one the symbols to which he is conditioned pass once again before his view as they did at his own initiation, charged with emotion as that experience must be for any sincere follower of the Mystery Tradition, that the associated images tend to form themselves in his mind into moving pictures of great clarity. The odd part is, however, that if notes come to be compared later on it will be found that the candidate, who has not yet been "conditioned" will, if he is at all responsive, be getting approximately the same mental pictures. If, in a higher degree, it is revealed that the senior brethren present, who sit silently throughout the ceremonial, are engaged in building definite mental pictures, he will begin to understand what is happening.

It will be found that if a person has been taught by ritual and meditation to associate a given symbol with a given force, then if that force, for want of a better term, might be said to impinge on his soul, the associated image will rise into consciousness if consciousness is not otherwise occupied. That is why Freud found that the subconscious content came to light during sleep; and for the same reason the trained initiate uses his power of concentration to make his mind a blank when he desires to perceive psychically.

Of course the same problem assails the psychic as perplexes the psycho-analyst, that is to say, *embarras de richesse*; but he has his own highly developed technique for solving it, and that technique lies in the conditioned symbol. Acquire a stock of carefully conditioned symbols, and when an influence impinges on consciousness, the appropriate symbol will rise with the accuracy of a signal flag.

The Qabalists, in pursuit of this principle, have reduced the universe to ten primary principles, which they call the Ten Holy Sephiroth; with each Sephirah are associated four colours, which represent the mode of functioning of its force from subtle to dense. Once these colours are firmly associated in the mind the forces assigned to their particular Sephirah, they are the first things that are thrown up onto the surface of consciousness when a subtle force of the corresponding type impinges on the mind. They come up as an idea of a colour, or even the colour itself, before any definite idea or concrete image presents itself to the mind.

The art of psychic development consists in catching these tenuous impressions as they flit past. The subconscious mind itself will clothe them in all manner of images drawn from its own depths both of personal experience and the inherited memories of the group-mind in which he shares; these, unless recognised traditional symbols, are personal to the observer, and constitute that *embarras de richesse* which is so highly embarrassing, both intrinsically and extrinsically. The more highly trained person will have additional and more precisely conditioned symbols available for his use, and the work of the Thirty-two Paths, as it is called, consists in building these and conditioning them. But however elaborate and precise a system may be, it is in the colouring that the key is to be found.

This colour system is found scattered in every direction throughout the literature of the Mysteries - the coloured wings of angels, the robes of the Masters, the symbols of the gods, the gems associated with the astrological signs, all these are compact of colour symbolism; and this symbolism, codified and arranged upon the Tree of Life, is the great key of the Mysteries. Students interested in the subject will find it tabulated and set out at the head of each section of my *Mystical Qabalah* to which, in the light of what I have said here, he should refer.

The art of practical psychic development, then, consists in the capacity to hold the mind steady and still, concentrated upon a given subject, and observe what rises to the surface. In actual practice that is achieved in the following way. The mind is concentrated upon a given idea to the exclusion of all else by means of some form of litany or ritual, when everything else has been left behind, the mind, still held to the idea, is stilled as far as possible, and what passes like wind over grass upon its still surface is first observed, and then analysed. If the work of conditioning the symbols has been well done, it is the symbols that will pass first across it under such conditions, and they are analysed and read off according to the tables given in *The Mystical Qabalah*. In this way it is possible to check up on one's psychic visions with a high degree of accuracy. True, there will be much subconscious content mixed in with the symbolism, but the symbolism, being based upon the innate nature of mind itself, and upon racial traditions as enshrined in the traditional group mind, will form a framework to the whole, and, like Ariadne's thread, enable us to find a way through the labyrinth of the psychological *embarras de richesse*.

The visions of the trained and initiated psychic are clear-cut and conventionalised; the visions, for the matter of that, of the experienced psychic, even if not initiated, tend to become conventionalised and develop a symbol system of their own, which is sometimes singularly close akin to the traditional one. The high water mark of psychic achievement is touched when the spontaneous dreams of sleep take on this conditioned symbolism and one experiences what are called "lucid dreams", that is to say, dreams that are like no other dreams in their powerful influence upon life and consciousness.

Another, and very curious application of the stylised dream remains to be noticed, and that is the phenomena to be obtained in the psychic trance, into which some persons fall spontaneously and into which the higher grades of adept can throw themselves at will. This trance is nothing more or less than auto-hypnosis, and the visions that arise therein are of the same nature as already described, that is to say, they are determined by influences, both subjective and objective in varying proportions, which work upon the raw material provided by the subconscious content, dramatising it into cartoons. This, and nothing else, is what has been called "travelling in the spirit vision", it is an induced dream, but a dream which is conditioned by influences beyond the subconscious content. The value and interest of these visions is very great provided we can be sure of getting away from our subconscious content into wider air and are not engaged in the salubrious occupation of chewing our own tails, which not infrequently happens to persons who are still bound to the wheel of desire.

Chapter 4b

PSYCHIC PERCEPTION
Gareth Knight

Psychic perception is a great deal more common than is realised. Indeed it is a faculty as universal as the imagination. Thus it should not be regarded as a special prerogative of certain select souls with "the second sight" or who are from a line of specially gifted forebears. As with any human faculty, natural ability will vary but there are very few who cannot benefit considerably from training.

It is, for the most part, a particular knack of using the imagination. This is usually for the most part in pictorial terms but the auditory imagination can also play an important role. It is the faculty that many successful novelists and playwrights develop and use. However, it can also have a formless aspect, in which case it may best be referred to as the intuition. That is to say, the direct perception of ideas that come into mind, as if they were our own.

This subjective/objective divide is a question common to all forms of inner perception. Are the pictures we see in the minds eye, the words we hear with the inner ear our own, or dropped there by an external agency? Or are we using the mind as a direct organ of perception independently of the physical eyes or physical ears to apprehend some inner but nonetheless objective reality?

The pragmatic approach is to leave such philosophical and psychological speculations aside and to concentrate on the experience. For that is where the proof of the pudding is likely to be. And we will soon learn by experience that the most effective way to encourage psychic perception is to believe in it implicitly.

This attitude may seem fraught with possibilities of self deception. However, giving all psychic perceptions the benefit of the doubt at the time of perceiving them does not mean to say that we should not subject them to later critical analysis.

Indeed the hall mark of the competent magician is to be able to switch freely and easily from one mode of mind-set to another. And in the course of time, an attitude of benevolent agnosticism can become the order of the day. Then when sufficiently strong links have been built up with inner sources of communication over a period of time, they can be challenged and questioned, just as two friends might converse or dispute, or a student question a teacher.

A negative or sceptical attitude will certainly shut down all perception stone dead. Just as a credulous and superstitious acceptance of all that comes into psychic purview will tend to dilute and degrade whatever was of value in the communication in the first place.

It is the development of genuine psychic perception that is the object of the individual meditation exercises, of going on imaginary journeys, describing imaginary scenes, conducting imaginary conversations. There will come a time when these imaginary actions become real, have an objectivity of their own.

This will still be within the sphere of the imagination. We are not looking for them to appear to be physically objective, for that would not be psychic perception but hallucination. Nor do we seek for uncontrolled interior visions, for that is not perception but delirium.

It is the possibility of these pathologies, very rare in normal circumstances, that make esoteric schools reluctant to take on students with a record of psychic instability. Practical occult work is not for those in need of psychotherapy, for some of its techniques are close to what in less fortunate circumstances can be the symptoms of schizophrenia. Although, conversely, it is not beyond the bounds of possibility that very sensitive natural psychics have been diagnosed and treated as schizophrenics.

For much the same reasons, responsible occultists will have no truck with drugs, and are cautious of them even when medicinally prescribed. The competent magical worker is always in control of the faculties of consciousness, even when their content may seem, by ordinary standards, remarkable.

In practical terms psychic over-sensitivity is the least of the average student's problems. This may be because the general climate of modern opinion is so sceptical that a great deal of psychological conditioning has to be sloughed off before we realise that we are not so psychically deaf and blind as we think.

This is another reason why ritual is a very useful discipline and training ground because the intensity of its methods are capable of bringing students on more quickly than working alone. When a functioning group meets it provides a focus of trained minds concentrating upon closely defined imagery within a well defined purpose. This will have a strong telepathic effect upon anyone who is sitting within that circle.

Added to this is the inner plane element, for the focused attention and imagery of the outer plane group will be as a strong magnet and beacon tower for inner energies and presences of a similar type, that are in sympathy with the work that is going forward. Thus the student practitioner is in a psychic atmosphere that is doubly concentrated, and within half a dozen meetings should be picking up individual psychic perceptions without too much trouble.

Within a magical working there will be an overall framework of what might be called "positive psychism". That is to say, specific images are described for all present to visualise. This framework may be an imagined journey to some temple or inner place of working. This is what is usually called a "composition of place" and its function is very much the same as what we have already described as a "composition of mood". Indeed the terms are almost synonymous; they bring into line the mood and imaginative content of all present. This has a powerful objective effect upon the subtle planes, in much the same way as in a magnet, which is simply a bar of iron in which all the individual atoms are induced to face the same way. They thus contribute to each other's influence to form a very perceptible magnetic field within another dimension.

In the Chapels of Remembrance working that we have briefly described, the basic shape and furniture of each chapel is the overall form for the working upon the psychic level. And this was matched, in somewhat simplified form, by symbolic objects and ritual furniture within the physical lodge.

The initial composition of place in this instance was a short descriptive journey from a scene at the outer gate into the containing building, in through its doors, and up to the war memorial inside, which marks the place of the entrance to the chapels.

We are standing at the outer gate of a great abbey church. Beyond its frame of ornate ironwork the wide stone-paved path invites us in towards the porch of the north door, flanked on either side by mature yew trees. We enter along this path, and as we make our way between the trees we are aware of the presence of the Masters of our Lodge, walking in the grounds on either side of the path. For they are always here, ready to provide advice, encouragement and assistance to all who come here seeking truth. Entering the porch, we approach the guardian at the door, to whom we each mentally speak our name so that we may be more readily identified by our inner plane brethren. He salutes each of us in turn and we pass through into the Abbey.

As our eyes grow accustomed to the low light inside this magnificent building, our attention is drawn to a large white tablet set into the wall in the south aisle, directly opposite to where we are standing. We make our way over to it, crossing the nave and passing the great font, and as we draw nearer we see that it is a war memorial. The white tablet is vast in size, covering much of the wall, and is of polished marble. Engraved over its entire surface are countless names, the names of those slain in the Great War, 1914-1918. This elegant roll-call is so enormous that it is only possible to read a tiny proportion of the names at one time, and most of them are unfamiliar, although you may see a few that you recognise. Underneath the tablet is a marble shelf, thickly strewn with poppies, and to one side is a rough wooden cross, salvaged from a soldier's makeshift grave on the battlefield. Although this memorial is ostensibly dedicated to those who fell in the Great War, it is implicitly honouring the victims of all wars. We stand before it for a moment, respectfully contemplating all that it represents.

This directed visualisation will have the effect of concentrating the minds of all present upon a particular set of symbolic images and at the same time set the general mood and intention of what is to follow. A natural extension to this build up of an inner place of working is to invoke, in the imagination, some kind of guardian and guide.

In this particular instance we have a comparatively well known, and appropriate figure, in the form of one of the leading war poets of the First World War, Wilfred Owen. Whether or not this is a direct evocation of the soul of a particular individual is not a question that we can usefully enter at this point. The intention in this case is not so much with the individual personality of the war poet but with his function, as representative of many thousands for whom he forms an appropriate figure head and mouthpiece. This is the difference between a spiritualist séance and a magical working. The séance aims for social interchange with a particular personality no longer in the flesh; the magical working operates more impersonally at the level of symbolic function. Although this does not mean to say that psychic impressions received on such occasions do not lack for personal warmth or feeling. But to return to the composition of place, of which an evocation of the guardian/guide forms a part:

We become aware of a figure standing nearby looking up at the marble tablet. He is a short, dark-haired young man wearing the uniform of an officer of the First World War. As if sensing our presence he turns round and greets us with a shy smile, and we recognise him as the poet Wilfred Owen. During his life he devoted much time to helping the poor and the sick, and he was working as a teacher when war broke out. He was deeply opposed to the principles of war but considered it his duty to enlist, and was sent to the front line with the 2nd Manchester Regiment. His experiences on the Somme caused him to have a breakdown, and it was while he was recovering from this that he wrote many of his finest and most powerful poems about the futility of war. In 1918 he returned to the front line voluntarily, where he won the Military Cross for conspicuous gallantry and was killed seven days before the Armistice, aged 25. It is now his duty and honour to guard the entrance to the Chapel of Remembrance, where he stands as an archetype of the pity of war, and he will serve as our guide on this pilgrimage.

He welcomes each of us in turn, and invites us to deepen our understanding of what is represented in the Chapel of Remembrance.

And in the context of the ritual some words of Owen were slightly adapted to summarise the intention and spirit of the ritual.

My subject is War, and the pity of War. The Poetry is in the pity. If the spirit of it survives, my ambition and those names will have achieved themselves fresher fields than Flanders.

And although the detail of much of the description is set in the context of the 1914-18 war, the intention of the ritual encompasses human warfare everywhere, in every place and time.

Thus among the psychic perceptions that individuals picked up on the occasion of first working this ritual there were resonances of the Gododdin poems written by the military bard Aneirin as elegies to those who fell at the battle of Catreath in about 600 A.D. Also a Cromwellian trooper from the time of the English Civil War turned up. Then two young men wearing SS uniform, very apprehensive, unarmed and very vivid indeed, who stayed by the one who observed them and would not move. And at the end a group of black GIs filed past carrying Vietnam era equipment, and seemed on their way somewhere as if the ritual had given them some place to go. One was whistling a Jimmy Hendrix number.

A number of those present received a strong psychic impression of the picture over the back of the altar in the second chapel. This was not of Owen but of another of his time and circumstance, who has been making contact with various magical workers over the past seventy years, and seems to be of the rank of Master in the esoteric scheme of things, although his communicating personality at times is not too far removed from a character in the pages of P.G.Wodehouse.

Several commented on how vividly this picture built up, and in particular the jocular attitude of the figure, who seemed to be leaning at a very jaunty angle upon his stick and grinning. This is an instance of where the "positive psychism" of the deliberately described and visualised image spills over into "perceptive psychism" in observing that image take on some kind of spontaneous action.

With regard to this, the initiate who conducted this rite (and who in a series of contacted meditations had taken down the bulk of it verbatim from this contact) later commented:

With reference to the photograph of D.C. on the wall of the Sacred Heart chapel, this was something he was very, very keen that I should include. The idea behind it is to strengthen the contacts that he has with group members, and the picture acts as a useful focus for this. A couple of people said afterwards that they had seen him wave his walking stick around and strike a silly pose; that is the hallmark of a genuine contact. So if any of you find him floating about on the periphery of your consciousness in the next few days or weeks, do follow it up and try to tune in to him - it's what he specifically wanted.

Chapter 5a

RITUAL INITIATION
Dion Fortune

There is, perhaps, no aspect of occultism upon which more foolishness is talked than upon ritual, whether initiatory or evocative. The very mention of ceremonial magic is enough to crisp the hair; but ceremonial magic is simply mind power concentrated and co-ordinated by means of a formula. It has its uses, and certain very definite applications, but it has also its limitations; and to think that a magician has only to wave a wand and say Abracadabra, or words to that effect, and all present will fall flat, is completely to misunderstand the modus operandi of ceremonial. It is safe to say that if a spy were present at even the most exalted ceremonial, far from being blasted, it is only curiosity that would save him from boredom. Equally, upon the other hand, it is folly to deny the power of ritual, but it is only powerful to affect the prepared mind, the mind of a person who has been "conditioned" to the symbols employed; we have already seen the amount of work that it takes to produce the necessary "conditioning". It is obvious therefore, that no casual observer will be even impressed, much less affected.

A person naturally psychic would receive definite psychic impressions, possibly so strong as to be unpleasant; but these would be chaotic in nature because he would not know what to look for, or how to receive that which he perceives. Consequently he would receive the influences of the ceremony in an unequilibrated manner, and his natural instinct would be to resist them. This would disturb the astral aspect of the ceremony, for it is very needful to be of one mind in one place for ceremonial, because the mind work is all important.

In dealing with subjects that are not generally familiar, a clearer impression is created by an ounce of concrete example than by many pounds of first principles. Let us then consider the way in which an initiate makes use of the technique of ceremonial, bearing always in mind that this technique is simply a means of concentrating mind power.

It is a matter in which everything depends upon the foundations laid in the preliminary training, unless the student has a firm grasp and an intelligent understanding of first principles, he will inevitably fall into either superstition or incredulity; of the two, the latter is much to be preferred, as it does no harm even if it does no good; but to credulity any follies are possible.

We have already indicated the foundations that need to be laid - a grasp of the esoteric philosophy and the conditioning of the mind to the standard symbols. The first is achieved by theoretical studies - the second by the successive experiences of the initiation ceremonies of the grades. In these ceremonies, trained people make the thought-forms and build up the atmosphere into which the newcomer is introduced; symbols are shown to him under such circumstances, and if he is at all responsive, he becomes definitely conditioned to them in the way already described. Consequently there will be certain symbols which for him will have the same power to affect his imagination ever after as have those that he learnt at his mother's knee when his mind was open and impressionable.

But it is not enough that a student goes through a ceremony once, and has done with it. He must work upon the symbols to which he has been introduced if their influence is to build up, and not fade out; for his mind no longer has the plasticity of infancy, except under conditions of intense emotion, which imprint upon a single exposure; consequently subsequent work has to be performed in order to consolidate what has been achieved.

To this end, the student practises daily meditation upon the symbols that have been communicated to him, and in any system worthy of the name he practises it in such a manner that everything is linked together into a synthetic whole and correlated about a central point. In the Jesuit system, for instance, it centres about the Passion of Our Lord; in the Hermetic aspect of the Western Esoteric Tradition everything is co-ordinated upon the Tree of Life. This I have explained in detail in my book *The Mystical Qabalah*, and I do not propose to make any mystery about it; that book, and these articles, taken together, explain the whole system. All that the student needs in addition are, firstly, the skill that comes from experience - and this is not communicable; and secondly, the contacting onto the actual thought-forms employed; this is reserved, because inexpert use of these thought-forms damages them.

By his daily meditations, then, the student expands and extends that which has been revealed to him. Gradually the symbols reveal their significance as he works at them; gradually he sees their relationship to his own life and its problems, soon he becomes expert at interpreting life's experience in terms of the symbol language of the Mysteries. Periodically he returns to watch the same ceremony being worked in which he received his original "conditioning", and renews the experience with more understanding, until at last he has arrived at a realisation of its significance and may be said to have completed the Degree. Then he goes on to the next, and the process is repeated with the additional material now available.

In this way he learns to realise himself as part of the cosmic whole; he learns to work with the technical methods of the Mysteries, and to contact the forces they are designed to bring through. All this is taught in a simple and elementary form, with the power well damped down, until the student acquires skill and is habituated to the influences, and gets over any reactions due to repressed complexes that he is likely to make; for if there are pathologies in his own soul, it is best that he should make his reactions and adjustments at a low voltage rather than a high one. Some reaction there always will be to every effectual initiation, for no-one is perfect, and all unbalanced force in his nature has its disequilibrium temporarily exaggerated by the influx of force concentrated by the ceremony; but it should be the reaction of an inoculation, not an actual outbreak of the disease.

If candidates are wisely chosen and properly prepared, this is what occurs. For at least a year the student's daily meditations are examined and checked, and at certain points in his course he is interviewed, and that interview is no perfunctory routine, but a careful investigation by experienced persons. Not very much gets through that is better kept out.

As no initiation fees are charged, there is no point in advancing an unsuitable person. Whether they are poor as church mice or rich as Croesus makes no difference; to admit unsuitable Croesuses would serve no useful purpose, as they would speedily depart in disgust, explaining to all who would listen that there is nothing in the system. Which we may as well admit, is the simple truth. There is nothing in the system except what the student puts into it in the way of work and intuition; and as I have so impolitely said of other people's systems, all the teaching can be collected from the shelves of second-hand bookshops or the popular translations of the classics. "The pearls are not mine, but only the thread on which they are strung."

As of old, the Outer Court leads into the Lesser Mysteries. In these the student learns the use of the occult technique. Neither original research nor the production of phenomena is encouraged here, but the student is made to stick to a system of work and discipline; everyone goes through the same course, and the many types of polygonal pegs have to accommodate themselves to the same round hole. This is done for two reasons, firstly, to ensure equilibrium of temperament by forcing a person to strengthen his weak points and curb his exuberances; and secondly, to put the stamp of a common discipline upon all members of the Fraternity, so that subsequent specialisation shall not lead to fission of the organisation or a development of a one-sided viewpoint in those who specialise. Even those who like the process least at the time can generally be found to agree that it has been salutary and has broadened the outlook and given an understanding of the point of view of other temperaments.

The Lesser Mystery training is exactly the same as the exercises that build up the muscles of a dancer or the hands of a pianist; it is the essential basis of all that follows and can be put to a multiplicity of purposes with equal efficacy. The same technique that enables a ministrant to administer the Eucharist with power also enables the alchemist to make that transmutation of the higher gold which is the Philosopher's Stone of the Illuminati.

Once this generalised technique has been acquired, specialisation becomes the order of the day. The classification is a simple psychological one into the three temperaments - the intellectual, the devotional, and the artistic, and even in these there is no hard and fast division, and the combination of two of the three is not only permitted, but encouraged. It is rare to find a student who can combine all three, and for practical reasons it is inadvisable to try to do so at one time, but to alternate between them.

The devotional and the artistic temperaments have their own special technique of training and operation, which will be considered elsewhere in due course; let us for the moment confine ourselves to the further developments of the Hermetic method, the Way of the Middle Path.

Employing the technique we have already described, the student works his way systematically through the Thirty-two

Paths of the *Sepher Yetzirah*, conditioning himself to their symbols. *Hoc opus, hic labor est.* Or in plain English, this will keep him busy for some time.

Now let us consider the use made of this knowledge and experience by those who, having completed the Paths, may justly be considered adepts. Firstly, such a one works upon his own soul, perfecting it, equilibrating, purifying and harmonising character; freeing himself from the bondage of imperious desires; strengthening and refining his intellectual powers, and stocking his mind with such learning as may bear upon his chosen subjects of specialisation.

At the same time he is establishing relationship between himself and the Cosmos; he is making himself part of a larger whole, living with its life, transmitting its energies, serving its purposes; it is this realisation that we do not live to ourselves alone as separate enclosed spheres of selfish interests, that is so all-important to the ethics of the Mysteries; but we cannot enter upon it at the moment as we are here only concerned with the practical technique. It is from this realisation, and this alone, that the power of the magus is derived; without it, for all his learning and self-discipline, he might as well cultivate cabbages.

Chapter 5b

RITUAL INITIATION
Gareth Knight

The general custom and practice within the Western Esoteric Tradition so far as the training of a ritual magician is concerned is a series of graded initiations, about which there is considerable glamorised speculation, perhaps encouraged by the colourful traditional nomenclature. The grades, however, are no more mysterious than high school grades and serve very much the same purpose.

Symbolic detail will vary from one organisation to another but generally speaking there is an Outer Court for the sifting and sorting out of general enquirers, followed by a system of Lesser Mysteries, very often with three formal grades. Beyond that lie the Greater Mysteries where progress and training tends to be on a more individual basis.

In the Lesser Mysteries the general basic techniques of ritual are acquired, including the inner preparation of the individual in the practice of meditation and guided or spontaneous visualisation. The Lesser Mysteries are likely to have what is called an Outer Court; an introductory stage usually conducted in the form of a correspondence course, for studying very basic theory and laying the groundwork of a meditation discipline. Those unable to sustain the simple discipline imposed will soon go their own way, to mutual benefit.

This is a stage of the game where many applicants are at the phase of spiritual awakening known as that of the Seeker.

They may well be very competent and dedicated souls who have in this life just received the inner call to seek the higher wisdom and are in the process of finding a teacher and a system of training that is suited to them. The Outer Court of the Lesser Mysteries enables the Seeker to see if this is the appropriate way without too much commitment on either side.

Progress through the Outer Court may take anything from a year to eighteen months, for anything less than this is unlikely to provide a sufficiently rigorous screening process. It is not unusual to expect a 90% drop out rate from an initial study course of this nature, but those who do pass through it are likely to have found what they have been seeking with some degree of certainty.

After successfully passing through the Outer Court and probably a personal interview where any outstanding doubts or problems may be aired by either party, the Neophyte can be admitted to the Lesser Mysteries. And in a ritual organisation this is likely to commence with a ritual initiation.

A ritual initiation is simply a ritual which is aimed to be of personal benefit to the Neophyte being admitted, and in a three degree Lesser Mystery system there will probably be an initiation for each grade or degree.

A ritual initiation, let it be said, is not an ordeal. Nor does it have anything to do with the humiliating of an individual, often with sexual connotations, that are the staple of many more public "initiation ceremonies", such as those associated with apprenticeship or entry to some closed group like the police or the military.

The purpose of initiation into a ritual training group is to introduce the candidate to the symbolism of the degree, and into the group mind of the body of people who currently constitute that degree. There will be a curriculum through which everyone works, along much the same lines as study in the Outer Court, but individual study will now be supplemented by attendance at group ritual and other meetings.

The precise symbolism of each degree curriculum is confidential to its members for this enables a tight group mind to be built, a psychic shell in which appropriate spiritual development can be encouraged and accelerated.

To reveal the precise details of the symbols and rituals to those outside the degree and group concerned would, to a large extent, cause a leakage of their power. However, the general principles are much the same throughout the general tradition and various systems have been published, as for example those of the Hermetic Order of the Golden Dawn and various Masonic rites. (Although very few Freemasons are ritual magicians, many of their rituals can be very powerful indeed if worked by trained minds, which suggests something about their origin, if not their current practice).

If we examine the structure of many of the published rituals we see a general pattern of pillars and altar, perhaps after the style of Solomon's Temple as described in the Biblical Book of Kings or the Chronicles, together with symbolic patterns set in a mosaic pavement within a chequered floor pattern. Two symbols of particular import for the initiate of the Lesser Mysteries may be in evidence, the rough and perfect ashlars. These signify that on entry to the Lesser Mysteries the soul of the candidate is like a rough stone just hewn from the quarry, but having passed through the degrees of the Lesser Mysteries will become as a stone that has been squared and polished, made symmetrical, and fitted with a ring bolt so that it can be hoisted to its appropriate place in the edifice of the temple. That temple of which the candidate aspires to form a part is the temple of the Greater Mysteries.

In various schools however, the nomenclature may differ slightly. In the Hermetic Order of the Golden Dawn, for instance, they used the term 1st Order, for the Lesser Mysteries, and 2nd Order, for the Greater, with a potential 3rd Order for those who had advanced sufficiently far in the Greater Mysteries. In other circles these latter categories might be termed the Outer and Inner Greater Mysteries. The word Mysteries is used in the same sense that it is defined in the Catholic Church, that is to say, a spiritual truth that is beyond the general processes of reason.

The candidate undergoing an initiation ceremony may be temporarily lightly bound and blindfolded. This is not part and parcel of any bondage fetish but a symbolic signification that the newcomer to the Mysteries comes seeking freedom and enlightenment. Having been freed from the blinds and encumbrances of the outer world the candidate is shown the appropriate symbolism of the degree, and given instruction by the ritual officers concerned, at various stations within the lodge. A promise of confidentiality and good faith is also given.

Traditional Masonic oaths have been couched in most violent and bloodthirsty terms and whilst there may be a certain justification in maintaining ancient traditions, according to a seventeenth or eighteenth century taste in such matters when some of these rituals were first written, such bizarre overstatements are generally a thing of the past. In practical terms in modern magical ritual practice one prefers to say what one means, and mean what one says.

The same applies to dark references to modes of tribulation such as "the Punitive Ray" that was dear to the hearts of some Victorian ritualists, concepts deserving more levity than fear. As in many walks of life, the more colourful the talk, the less the real threat, for real power has no need of braggadocio.

Even so, it should be said that breaking faith with the Mysteries in any significant way is not a matter to be undertaken lightly. But this is not so much a matter of punishments being meted by vengeful spirits but more in the way of powerful pent up forces being released in an unbalanced manner by unbalanced attitudes, which can indeed give a rough ride to the malevolently disaffected.

One welcome change in modern esoteric attitudes is that groups may divide and go their separate ways without vituperation and mutual condemnation for being schismatics.

It being more widely recognised that groups may seed like dandelion clocks. According to their purpose, they have an optimum size, beyond which division may be welcome if not a necessity. Whatever overall occult unity that is required has its base upon the inner planes.

In general terms the three grades of the Lesser Mysteries are divided by natural function. The Theoricus within the 1st Degree studies the general alphabet and theory of the Mysteries, such as, for example, elementary Qabalah and the symbolic correspondences of the Tree of Life and various branches of mythopoeic story and legend. The Practicus within the 2nd Degree should be more concerned with building these symbolic artefacts, both physically and within the mind, perhaps constructing a personal ritual temple or shrine and collecting together a personal armamentarium of ritual equipment. The Philosophus within the 3rd Degree should be proceeding to the use of these artefacts as a means of personal conscious contact with the invisible realities. And these should be realities indeed, and not just glamorous hypotheses linked to various symbolic play-things.

The achieved initiate of the 3rd Degree should therefore be a pretty competent magician and may well elect to stay at this particular level, a skilled server of the mystery lodge of which he or she forms a part. "A hewer of wood and drawer of water" in the traditional phraseology, but a particularly skilled one at that, for the waters are those of higher consciousness, and the wood the wisdom framework of the Tree of Life.

However, it may fall to some to be called to more dedicated and individual service, which implies entry into the Greater Mysteries. This requires a personal dedication that should be as serious and binding as any sacrament or oath of allegiance on entry to a religious order. The initiation consists of what is sometimes called the Unreserved Dedication. This dedication is made to powers beyond the physical plane, to what is sometimes called the Planetary Hierarchy of Masters, or the Great White

Lodge - no outer label being entirely satisfactory. However, by the time the initiate is ready to make such a dedication there will, or should be, a vivid personal realisation as to just what exactly is being offered, and to whom, and to what purpose.

The Unreserved Dedication should not be offered lightly, and by this token it is not accepted lightly either, for "many are called but few are chosen". Any such dedication, whether or not accompanied by ritual initiation, has to be ratified by those upon the inner planes to whom the dedication is offered.

In the terminology of the Western Mystery Tradition, whosoever is so accepted is regarded as an Adept. There are indeed various grades of adept but at the level of the Greater Mysteries advancement is more a matter of individual training and the undertaking of specific tasks initiated from the inner planes. Indeed, another way at looking at this process is to regard the progress of the Adept as being one whose task it is to become more and more closely aware of the consciousness of a particular Master or Masters. The term "Master" should not be taken in the sense of "master and servant" even though mutual service is a criterion of work in the Mysteries. The relationship is more of the nature of inner guide, philosopher and friend.

A ritual initiation at the level of admission to Adeptus Minor is likely to be along the lines of a personal death and resurrection drama - for that is what is intended. The Dedicand is offering to give up the personality values of life in the outer world, and to be re-born to the values of the inner world.

This does not necessarily imply that the Adept must be free of all family and social ties and responsibilities. These, such as they may be, will remain and by the fact of the Unreserved Dedication be the greater cemented and sanctified. It is the greatest treason for the initiate to presume to sacrifice others in the outer world for assumed spiritual ideals. But allegiance to the work of the Masters comes second only to normal obligations to dependants, whether children, espoused, or aged. There is no place for high minded inhumanity in the Mysteries. That indeed is a short cut to the Left Hand Path, and one often well garnished with hypocrisy.

In the course of time the Adeptus Minor may be given greater responsibility and initiatives and this leads gradually to the grade of Adeptus Major. And one who is completely free by personal circumstance of outer ties and obligations, and who has the ability to function fully as an adept upon the physical plane, may be regarded as an Adeptus Exemptus. Needless to say their ranks are few and nor do they advertise themselves.

Generally speaking the higher grades are inner plane functions related to outer plane groups. The Masters or Inner Plane Adepti working behind a group may well be regarded as the Magestri Templi - the Masters of the Temple. The term Magus is an honorific one held by anyone who functions in office by running a ritual or a group upon the physical plane, but in terms of esoteric rank is confined to the Higher Masters, some few of whom, who specialise in teaching, are known by name and tradition. The term Ipsissimus may be considered as a unique role as its meaning implies.

The grades we have been describing are active functions and it may well be that some schools or study groups use similar titles in a much looser fashion. That is a matter for their own realisation and responsibility. Esoteric schools and societies with grand sounding names and titles are harmless enough, and may well do some good at their own level, even if the gap between function and title is a wide one.

Much of this may seem the excuse for some kind of élitism but this would be a misconception. The world is not divided between adepts and initiates on the one hand and the poor benighted "once-born" on the other. In terms of function there are some highly impressive human beings around who have no need of esoteric grades to make the world a better place. Magic is but one specialism among many. A specialism that is somewhat misunderstood in our day and age - but not one that necessarily confers any superiority in spiritual or moral terms over others. Any more than, in its true function, is it a fantasy refuge for those who cannot cope with the outer world.

Chapter 6a

THE REALITY OF THE SUBTLE PLANES
Dion Fortune

We have shown how subtle spiritual forces are rendered concrete, and therefore perceptible, by visualising them in the imagination as having forms. It is a moot question how far these actual forms thus visualised are formulated in the astral light and have a definite objective existence, outside the consciousness. There are many instances on record where psychics claim to have perceived them, but these instances are capable of more than one interpretation. It is extremely difficult either to prove or disprove anything in matters of psychism, for so many factors enter in over which we have no control, and the simple and all-pervading factor of telepathy may vitiate everything, reducing all so-called objectivity to a matter of subjectivity telepathically transferred. Nevertheless, so wide a field is opened up in this manner that we need reject nothing on this account, though it will necessarily modify our mode of approach and our estimate of the results obtained. For indeed if we have found a sure and certain manner of inducing given states of consciousness at will, we have found something exceedingly valuable. There is a subjective objectivity, if the term may be forgiven, in which the images in consciousness take on power and become self-moving; we see this happen with compulsive ideas in psychopathology; something of the same mechanism may be at work in certain magical phenomena; though even if it is, far from detracting from their value, it is enhanced, for many practical applications open up. It is a well-known maxim in magic that a basis of manifestation has to be provided for the spirit that is invoked to visible appearance; I have always maintained that the spirit exerts its influence upon the operator's personality, and he himself is the basis of evocation, whether the manifestation takes place in all the tangibility of ectoplasm, or more subtly, as magnetic or mind power.

The metaphysics of these thought-forms, ensouled as artificial elementals, is very complex, but for all practical purposes the operator acts "as if" they were objective, and induces in himself the same feelings of awe and devotion and self-confidence that he would have if they really were what he presumes them to be; and as the essence of the operation lies in the mind of the magician, he is unwise to look even a spiritual gift-horse too closely in the mouth. Be that as it may, extraordinary things can be done with these thought-forms, whether one can prove their objective existence or not. They serve their purpose of concentrating subtle and specialised forces in a very effectual manner, which, so far as my experience goes, can be equalled in no other way.

Whatever may be said concerning these forms, the forces they serve to concentrate are indisputable, though again it may be argued that we are simply freeing subconscious energies by their use. Now it is axiomatic that a rose by any other name would smell as sweet, and as it is our confidence in these cosmic forces that enables us to make use of them, we are unwise, for practical purposes, to split hairs in the matter of metaphysics. If we find it inhibits our powers if we believe these forces to be subconscious, for God's sake let us believe in God. If, on the other hand we, being congenitally sceptical, feel we are making fools of ourselves if we hold any such beliefs, then let us confide in the subconscious if we have confidence in it. Neither party, so far as I know, can prove anything, or disprove anything, on the data available it is simply a matter of opinion.

So far as my personal opinion goes, I may say that it appears to me that the subconscious element is unquestionably very large, but that I find it hard to explain some of the experiences I have both had and seen on the assumption that it is subconsciousness and nothing more. I have always believed that by utilising the subconscious element in our minds we are able to gain access to other planes of existence. Let us, then, accept the subconscious, of whose ways we know a good deal, as our basis, but let us regard it as a means to an end and not an end in itself.

Approaching the matter thus temperately, we are enabled to make a start and learn by experience. Whereas if we were to accept as axiomatic the objectivity of the subtle planes, we might reject the whole concept from lack of knowledge of its implications. By going to work "as if" it had objective existence and could exert influence, we obtain results; it is noteworthy that the more confidence a person has in its objective existence, the better results he obtains. As Our Lord said, "According to your faith, be it unto you."

The whole question of the reality of the subtle planes, and the objectivity of the experiences related thereto, presents a nice problem in philosophy, and one profitably to exercise the powers of philosophers. If we accept matter, with its weight and occupation of space as our standard of reality, of course we must deny objective existence to the subtle planes; but who accepts such a standard nowadays? Only the very naive. Modern physics has pushed matter itself right off the plane of reality if it is to be judged by these standards, and the unhappy materialist sees his standard disappearing along with that which he is applying it to.

Our problem, then, is the old one that beset Bishop Berkeley - does anything exist outside the mind of the thinker? Would blue still be blue if no one knew it was blue? Like the old problem as to which came first, the hen or the egg, it is not only very abstract, but also very practical.

Do the phenomena of the subtle planes, which we perceive psychically, exist apart from the consciousness of the mind perceiving them? Are we, when we observe the inner planes with our psychic vision, simply looking into our own subconsciousnesses? The sceptic says we are, and thinks he has disposed of us. But has he? Do we ever perceive anything except our own mental content? Surely it is a manufactured product that consciousness is aware of when the mind says it sees. Do we not all, like the Lady of Shalott, gaze into a subjective magic mirror? People have been found to argue that this is the case, nevertheless, they eat the dinner reflected in their magic mirror, just as Christian Scientists treat the non-existent matter for its complaints and judge results by the changes in that which isn't there. I have yet to meet the idealist in philosophy who lived up to his ideals.

Perhaps the truth of the matter lies, as usual, in a combination of both view-points. What the Lady of Shalott sees is not objective reality, but the play of light and shade in her mirror; but there is something beyond her island that is causing the play of light and shade. Therefore life for her does not begin and end in her mirror; nevertheless, everything for her depends upon the focus of her mirror, so for practical purposes the idealists have the last word. The old occultists, in their dogmatic fashion, had a great deal to say about what they called the "sphere of sensation", and attached great importance to it. Now this sphere of sensation is none other than the magic mirror of the Lady of Shalott. The sphere of sensation is, up to a point, an effective buffer State between us and objective reality on all planes, as the Christian Scientists have discovered, though they call their discovery by the name of divine healing. Beyond that point, reality takes charge and obtrudes itself, and the divine healer ends up in the coroner's court. This is a matter of experience, and as such, not arguable.

So then, we may say, that all things objective are reflected into our magic mirror, the sphere of sensation, and that in the management of that mirror, its focusing and directing and burnishing, we have much to say, but there can be objective influences so widespread and potent that turn our mirror how we will, we cannot dodge them; thus does such a universal fact as death obtrude itself upon the magic mirror of that practical idealistic philosopher, the Christian Scientist. There are also classes of objective phenomena so remote from our normal spheres of sensation that we never glimpse them unless we are at pains to focus the mirror upon them. These are the subtle planes and the psychism which perceives them.

Now it may well be, as the philosophers are never tired of rubbing into us, that the abbot on his ambling pad may be something quite different from what we perceive in the magic mirror. For instance, if our mirror be of a bluish tint, the scarlet abbot may appear purple; or if the Lady of Shalott was of Lollard tendencies, a perfectly amiable old gentleman may appear as a horned devil. For all practical purposes, the sphere of sensation is our sphere of operation, and colours all that comes into it with its own hue, and to a great extent can inhibit the entrance of anything alien and unacceptable. In this matter, however, it obeys laws that belong to the whole man, not his surface consciousness only, and the majority decisions of the complexes can, and frequently do, give verdicts that startle the man he thinks himself to be: hence the alleged independent action of the sphere of sensation.

Let us grant, then, the objectivity of the things that throw the images, and the subjectivity of the sphere of sensation, and then ask ourselves what about it? We shall see that the sphere of sensation, if constricted, cramps our style enormously; but, being subjective, and therefore under our control provided we are able to control ourselves, and this is not as common a power as might be imagined, the sphere of sensation is capable of indefinite expansion; only limited, in fact, by our capacity to realise the possibilities of the objective universe in which we play so infinitesimal a part. It is the expansion of this sphere of sensation which is the end envisaged by the Mystery methods.

Our spheres of sensation being entirely private affairs, and a primrose by the river's brim meaning one thing to the poet and another to the scientist, it follows that what we are pleased to call reality might bear little enough relationship to some of its representations in such magic mirrors as one sees in side-shows, where one pays sixpence for the privilege of laughing at oneself - a thing one's friends would be pleased to do for one free of charge. If we take the representations in our magic mirrors as God's last word on the subject of creation, we shall naturally err, and the sceptical will be able to poke holes in our statements. If, however, we realise how much of the effect obtained in a magic mirror depends upon the handling of it, we shall be achieving a nice balance between the subjective and the objective factors in our problem, and perhaps be on the way to reconcile the viewpoints of the idealists and the realists, both of whom have a lot of reason on their side even if truth will not die with either of them.

Now let us return once more to practical considerations, but this time we shall know much better where we stand. The occultist says, for all practical purposes all I can know is my own sphere of sensation, therefore I take that as my sphere of operation. I know that I can do a very great deal with my magic mirror in the way of focusing and burnishing, and I have been at great pains to achieve a technique for doing this effectually; this technique I call initiation.

No-one knows better than he does, if, that is, he has been properly trained, that the sphere of sensation is subjective; he is under no delusion that the images he sees therein are the actual things they represent; he also knows, however, that they must be a working approximation to the things they represent or he will not be able to adapt himself to his environment, and so will become extinct. But, and this is the real key to the doctrine of the sphere of sensation and its relation to objective reality, he knows that the images seen therein, although so far as they go, they correspond to reality, are only a selection of reality, and the selection may be so biased and incomplete as to distort reality into utter unreality. The subjective world differs from the objective in degree, not in kind; it differs in being a part and not a whole, and it is its incompleteness which makes it a fallen world. St. Paul expressed the hope that someday he would know even as he was known, and this is the hope of every initiate, and the end towards which he/she directs his/her efforts.

Chapter 6b

THE REALITY OF THE SUBTLE PLANES
Gareth Knight

There would not be a great deal of point in performing ritual magic if there were no such thing as the reality of the subtle planes. It would be no more than subjective amateur dramatics in a symbolic junk shop and for any who simply go through the motions of what they conceive to be ritual magic without adequate training, the same remarks apply.

An example of this is the reference made by Dion Fortune to the "ghost hunter" Harry Price, now probably forgotten but a minor sensation at the time, at any rate in terms of personal publicity. He performed a ritual from a medieval grimoire, complete with goat, on a mountain, to no perceptible result. A foregone conclusion as any ritual magician could have told him at the time. Although, given the dubious and fragmented nature of much of this old lore, he was probably fortunate to be saved from results by his own lack of competence.

The ability to contact the subtle planes, and to work effectively with a foot in both worlds, is also the hallmark of what is known as a "contacted" group. A group that is not "contacted" may be very effective as a discussion group, or as a school of occult theory, and its leader may well be strongly contacted to a certain degree, but unless capable of illumining that contact in others, then the group is not one that can initiate, or function as a conduit of power or teaching between the planes.

The way to the subtle planes however is always open, and the opening of the gates, even for an isolated individual, largely a matter of persistence, dedication and right motive. "Ask and you shall receive, seek and you shall find, knock and it will be opened to you" is a very true and powerful adage in the mysteries as in religious dynamics. It is surprising how few are prepared to take it at face value.

It may of course take patience. Contact with the forces of the subtle planes may not at first be conscious, but they will develop in time. Although in this period one of the principal difficulties for the neophyte is recognising the subtle contacts for what they are. Until then, the forces of the subtle planes may well be having a powerful effect upon the personality but simply being registered as swings of mood or other subjective states.

It is this that accounts for occasional strong irrational antipathies or heady romantic attachments of the type that some psychologists know as "projections" or "transference". Inner forces are being projected or transferred onto a convenient external hook upon the physical plane. These are instances of extremes, but the subtle planes make their presence felt in many lesser ways, sometimes euphoric, at other times in more depressive ways in terms of mood. In one sense this is part of the training, the finding and maintaining of personal equilibrium in the face of inner tides and winds, and discerning what is truly objective or subjective.

One fairly reliable sign that it is the winds and tides of the subtle planes that are the cause of an upset will be the lack of proportion between the emotional reaction and its apparent physical cause. Over-reaction is always a tell tale sign. And although part of the problem may be a defect of temperament it is a function of mystery training to try to sort these things out, or at least to measure their degree, and so we are sometimes put to the test. Thus any particular problem may not be of evil provenance, but simply the potter testing his artefact by giving it a ringing clout. In the symbolic terms of the rough and smooth ashlar, to which we have already referred, a fair amount of knocking off rough corners and grinding and polishing is part of the process of preparation.

In the end, however, the reality of the subtle planes is measured by the quality of the beings we contact there and the standard of our channels of communication. In some schools this is referred to as a process of tuning consciousness, in others it is described as a process of merging one's own with the master's aura. The diverse terms mean much the same thing.

In any teaching that is received it is not necessarily the meaning of the text that is of prime value. This may seem an odd concept, but in some instances, particularly with higher contacts, the real teaching and its benefit comes from the contact itself. The words (which may, when analysed, be largely pious truisms) simply being a means to obtain and maintain attention, while a larger, formless, intuitive or spiritual contact is implanted.

There is also a marked difference between the type of contact met with in spiritualist circles and those in a magical context. The former are more in the nature of social contacts, very little different from those in the outer world. The magical contact is more of a high powered affair, probably from one who has been through all the grades of the mysteries to take up a position of power and responsibility upon the inner planes. Such are sometimes called masters, sometimes inner plane adepti, sometimes simply guides.

However, although these magical contacts may prove to be more exalted in certain ways than the shades of our physical friends and relations, they are certainly not meant to be worshipped. Nor, while they may earn our respect, are they necessarily to be placed upon a lofty pedestal and revered. They come as teachers and friends, and like all good teachers and friends, all they seek of us is an effective working relationship.

Let us quote from a conversation between such an inner contact and an outer plane student in the early stages of interchange:

Student: *You mentioned last time that we both need to have unfuddled minds in order to embark on the next phase of work. Do Masters' minds get fuddled?*

Master: *Oh yes. Not in the same way that yours does, admittedly, but it is quite possible for me to become depleted and not function at 100%. We are not perfect, whatever some like to think.*

S: *That's an interesting point. If the Masters are not perfect then on whose authority are we following them?*

M: *Tell me, would you want me to be perfect?*

S: *No. If you were absolutely perfect then you wouldn't be "human" and I would find it much more difficult to relate to you.*

M: *Good, I'm glad you said that. God is perfect, and the Masters are not God. I cannot make you understand exactly what our status is in the cosmic scheme of things, so you will have to make do with more analogies I'm afraid. As an adult human being you have a certain way of thinking, an objective, slightly cynical way of thinking. In order to understand the status of the Masters a little better you need to regress a little, resume the unconditional mentality of childhood. Imagine yourself as a small child in an overwhelming situation - lost in a wood, or jostled in a city street. You are frightened and feel helpless, even if you are not in any immediate danger. Then along comes a grown-up, either a parent or a teacher or a family friend, who takes you by the hand and guides you. As a child, with a child's mentality, you don't stop to consider the personal merits or faults of that grown-up. You don't complain that they are imperfect (even though they inevitably are), that they have no authority to guide you when they are not necessarily much better than you are. No, you put your faith in them and go with them, and you are deeply comforted by their presence. For the simple reason that if they are imperfect they are nevertheless somewhat wiser and more mature than you are, and - most importantly - they are motivated by love. They won't lead you astray, and won't allow any harm to come to you, because they* *care about you and want to protect you, and make themselves responsible for your welfare. Your relationship with the Masters must be conducted along similar lines if you are going to be of any great service to the Work. It's no use trying to analyse our fallibility and question our authority - such suspicions achieve nothing. You just have to let us take you by the hand and guide you, in the belief that we know what we are doing a little bit better than you do, and that our motivation is rooted firmly in love.*

In another exchange the importance of faith and the avoidance of destructive intellectual analysis was emphasised. This was in relation to a vision that the questioner had had as a preliminary to the Chapel of Remembrance work.

S: There's something I don't understand about inner plane contacts. Why are they always with famous people? Was it really Wilfred Owen I saw?

M: Right, now we've got an example to illustrate two of my earlier points. The importance of faith and how unhelpful ideas and prejudices can be quite a major interference factor in these matters. Were you thinking about Wilfred Owen particularly when you were doing the meditation?

S: I wasn't thinking about him at all, that's why it surprised me.

M: Good, that's a start. Now what was your first thought when you saw him?

S: I thought - this must be an interjection from my own mind.

M: Why?

S: Because I couldn't see any earthly reason why W.O. should want to contact me - if indeed such contact were possible.

M: And what did he say to you?

S: Almost nothing. I saw him clearly enough, but it seemed he was not able to speak to me - he just stood there and looked at me.

M: And how did you interpret that?

S: I took it as evidence that it wasn't really him. If he really was there and wanted to communicate something then surely he would have done so.

*M: **WRONG!** Slide down the snake and miss a turn. Suppose I were to tell you that Wilfred Owen had every intention of communicating with you but **YOU wouldn't let him.** Is it surprising that he just stood there without saying much when lack of faith, as I told you, is an insuperable barrier to communication? How the hell is a chap supposed to have an intelligible conversation with somebody who refuses to believe in him? Refuses to believe in him when he's standing right there in front of them! How would you like it if you went to meet a new friend and they took one look at you and said "nah, not talking to you, I don't believe you really exist." Poor Wilfred!*

S: You're making me feel guilty now!

*M: So you should be! It's simple esoteric good manners to give somebody the credit for objective existence. It's just as daft to dismiss an inner plane contact as the product of a defective imagination as it would be to dismiss an outer plane contact as the product of a defective optic nerve. For that matter, one might play devil's advocate and ask how does Wilfred Owen know that you exist? You weren't even born until fifty years after his death, so you're occupying a time which was never in his consciousness. At least you can look with hindsight and know that he did exist in the material world at a particular time. He can have no such reassurance of your existence. Indeed, one might be surprised that he has any **concept** of your existence.*

S: Is there any way I can correct this error now that I've made it?

M: B-E-L-I-E-V-E.

S: I've always had this kind of instinctive moral idea that it's fundamentally wrong to call people who are dead, that one should always let them make the approaches. Would it therefore be wrong for me to try to contact W.O.?

M: I see no harm in it, since he approached you first. Just build up the image of him, (should be easier for you to see him than it is for you to see me, what with all the photographs that have survived) and he will come along to animate it if he's inclined to do so. I don't think he'll hold it against you that you slighted him last time. We're quite used to the problems of trying to get stuff rammed through to incarnate souls. Such a faithless lot!

This particular Master, who first contacted Dion Fortune in 1923, happens to have the personality, at least for purposes of communication, of another British officer of the 1st World War. It may be fitting to conclude this chapter upon the reality of the subtle planes by a personal reference to his status.

S: There's one thing I have to ask you, although I understand that you don't much like to be quizzed about it. There is a rumour (originating, as far as I can see, from Alan Richardson's biography of Dion Fortune) that David-Carstairs-the-young-officer-in-the-Great-War did not exist.

Well, is it true?

M: Ooh, slander! What a thing to confront a chap with! To accuse him to his face (so to speak) of being non-existent! We want Flanders, not slanders. Of course I really exist, you silly ass! Where do you think I got this personality, if I didn't incarnate in it? Do you think I just biffed along to the Personality Shop and said "I'll take an army surplus one, please, with a cheerful demeanour, and ideally a tragic early death to go with it. That should get 'em feeling nice and sorry for me." No, no, no, child, it doesn't work like that. (I'm being facetious, by the way, in calling you 'child' - you are twenty-seven; I was only twenty-four. There, that's a little snippet of biographical information that you didn't know before, isn't it?) And it's no coincidence that all the Masters ended their last incarnations with willing and honourable 'deaths' - it's a hallmark of a mature soul; think about that. I could not just assume a personality that did not belong to me, that did not develop through my own use of it. Remember what I said about personalities being coloured by the soul that shines through them. If this was not a genuine personality then you would know; its falseness would be obvious, you would not be able to feel the level of rapport and camaraderie that we have established. Besides which, I would be very little use as a communicator with humans if I did not have the benefit of human understanding and experience. Let me assure you, my personality is genuine. If I am a little hard to trace in terms of documentary evidence then that is no bad thing - there is nothing to be gained by taking the retrospective view, interesting though it may be to you. Maybe one day I will tell you more, to satisfy your curiosity, but for the moment you must work with me as I am, not as I was.

"Work with me as I am, not as I was" seems a fitting injunction for all who seek to work with those on the subtle planes. And also perhaps a caution about any egocentric concern with our own status in previous incarnations. All we have and need for further progress is here now. We are the fruit of our past - the seed of our future.

Chapter 7a

FOCUSING THE MAGIC MIRROR
Dion Fortune

Let us grant, then, that the world as we know it consists of what is reflected in our magic mirror, and is built up into images in that treasure house of images, the sphere of sensation. The objective reality, we shall find, is not intrusive, in fact, it is we who collide with it, not it that seeks us out, and it will leave us to stew in our own juice indefinitely for all the effort it will make to assert itself. We shall find then, that in our sphere of sensation we have scope for a very great deal of activity, and that here is a world that we can remake nearer to the heart's desire according to our energy and discretion, though how we will like it when we have remade it is another question; anyway, we have no need to endure it if we do not like it, but can get to work on it with every hope of results.

If, of course, we believe the sphere of sensation to be identical with objective reality, we shall sit down under it and accept our lot as inevitable; but if we realise the lesson of the Mysteries, that our environment as we know it is subjective, being our sphere of sensation, and that our magic mirror has exercised a completely overruling influence in selecting what images shall appear in that mirror, we shall see that we can modify our sphere of sensation in proportion to our power to re-focus the mirror, or in other words, to change our standpoint.

The difficulty in the way of making this change is inherent in the mind itself, and not in the environment. The mind is a creature of most rigid habit, and its ways are only changed in the same way that the acrobat extends the normal limitation of his sinews by patient exercise that little by little stretches them till they will accommodate themselves to the desired position. This is not done in a day, and because an effort of the will cannot do it, we jump to the conclusion that it cannot be done and that we must accept our fate as inevitable, and the contents of our sphere of sensation as corresponding accurately to objective reality; we do not allow for what can be accomplished by the cumulative effect of repeated efforts. Because, with one spraining wrench our legs cannot be made to do the splits, we say the splits are impossible to the human form, and if some trained gymnast exhibits them in front of us in all their skilful gracelessness, we say like the small boy when he saw the giraffe at the Zoo, "I don't believe it"; or at best attribute the phenomena to the intervention of spirits.

If we would realise that the objective is real but unobtrusive, we would understand the problem of Berkeleyian idealism. If we would realise the tremendous adaptability of the sphere of sensation, provided we would treat it as the gymnast treats his limbs, with graduated exercises, and not as the bone-setter treats them, with brute force, we would soon discover what tremendous possibilities the subjective mind contains. It is these possibilities which are the subject of the research work of practical occultism; it is the application of them which constitutes the basis of magic and psychism. We are all the time manipulating the sphere of sensation; but because the sphere of sensation is all-important to us, and objective reality so unobtrusive, we have here a field so extensive that it is difficult to set any limit to its possibilities, always remembering, (a) that the work has to be done gradually, and (b), that objective reality imposes definite though amazingly wide limits within which we must work, and that if we transcend these limits, we shall collide with objective reality and find it hard, and turn our magic mirror how we will, we shall not be able to evade it.

The real sphere of the operation of the occultist lies in the selective capacity of the magic mirror, so that he can choose to a very great extent with what images he will people his sphere of sensation. In this he is one with the Christian Scientists; but unlike the Christian Scientists, he recognises the ultimate limits imposed by objective reality, and being a wise man, he bows to them and keeps out of the coroner's court.

But even within this limitation of infinity, much can be done; and it is the enormous amount that has and can be done which constitutes the occult tradition. The initiate, then, goes to work in his own sphere of sensation, and he may say to himself: "Something is lacking here", or "Something is inconveniently redundant there", and decide to make changes. This is called magic.

He knows that the thing he must aim at is equilibrium of forces, and that redundancies are best equilibrated by concentrating upon their opposite number. So he considers what will best equilibrate his redundancy or supplement his lack as the case may be, and he decides, according to such wisdom as he may possess, that such and such an influence would meet his need. If he is trained on the Qabalah, he expresses his ideas in terms of the Tree of Life, which is expressly designed to enable him to do so, briefly and comprehensively.

He knows that any given force is lacking or redundant on account of the selective action of the mirror, and that objective reality is there all the time, even if not obtruding itself. It is, in fact, this peculiar passivity of objective reality in relation to ourselves that is so surprising, for it is the exact opposite of what one has always been accustomed to believe. It is, however, as the psychoanalysts have discovered, and the Christian Scientists have used without discovering, that if you change a man's state of consciousness, you can bring about profound modifications in what he is pleased to call his environment, but which is really his sphere of sensation, his environment remaining constant all the time, as it always has been and always will be, and his selective activity alone being modified; but even that, thank God, goes a very long way.

Let us now consider the practical problem of altering the selectivity of the magic mirror, and consequently the contents of the sphere of sensation. I will not argue metaphysics any longer, but tell what is done by the operative occultist when he embarks upon the operation which is none other than magic. He knows by experience, and this is a point we cannot argue, but can demonstrate experimentally, that just as a given influence from the objective world will produce approximately the same images in all magic mirrors, blurred in some, distorted in others, clear-cut in a few, but always recognisable for what it is meant to be, so the building up of an image in the sphere of sensation will attract to it the corresponding influence from reality. How this works, we do not know, but we do know that it works within the limitation of natural law, and that it forms the basis of sympathetic magic.

Sympathetic magic is indeed a crazy and superstitious affair when applied to the alteration of objective reality, but when applied to the sphere of sensation it is quite another matter; it is, in fact, the kindergarten principle of "learning by doing", or as St. Ignatius Loyola told his Jesuits, "Put yourself in the attitude of prayer, and you will soon feel like praying." Make a suitable image in the sphere of sensation, and it will soon attract the corresponding force into your life.

These images are made with the pictorial imagination, and that is the reason why we train it so carefully in our meditation exercises, for it is to form the basis of future magical work.

These magical images, however, cannot be made just anyhow, even with intention, and obtain adequate results. They have to be adapted to the force they are intended to attract, and they have in consequence an elaborate technique. The occultist does not content himself with saying "Every day in every way I get better and better," and leaving it at that, though this is a good deal better than nothing, for subconscious intention takes the matter in hand, and in many cases delivers the goods, provided they are in stock; but if something more elaborate is required than the simple stock-in-trade of human harmony, more elaborate methods are necessary in order to obtain a clear-cut focus and concentration.

These methods have all been worked out in the greatest detail by the generations of initiates who have made use of them. There are different techniques in different traditions; for instance, the Eastern Tradition uses a technique which it calls yoga, which differs in many respects from that which we use in the West, and which we call magic, though the principles are the same. The differences are due to differences in temperament and training, not to any fundamental divergence of principle.

The modern Western occultist takes the Qabalah as his basis, and codifies all his systems around it, for the Western Tradition is a synthetic tradition, and is made up out of the converging streams of Greek, Egyptian and Chaldean influence.

When a Western initiate wants to construct in his sphere of sensation an image of a particular type, he refers to the tables of symbols that are associated with the Tree of Life; these are given in my *Mystical Qabalah* in relation to each of the stations on the Tree. From these he picks out the one that he feels to be suited to his purpose. If he lacks courage and energy, he would choose Geburah, the Sphere of Mars. If his problems concern the love-life, he would choose Netzach, the Sphere of Venus; if he wants spiritual illumination, the sphere chosen would be that of Tiphareth, the Sun. If he wants magical power, he would work with Yesod, the Moon-sphere. These things are not fool-proof, as is the simple method of prayer and devotion; the results he obtains depend upon his judgement in choosing and his skill in using. If he invokes Geburah for more strength in the fight, when what is really needed is the stabilising influence of Gedulah, or Chesed, the Sphere of Jupiter, the benign lawgiver, then he will find himself coming into touch with the destructive aspect of Geburah, and will learn some bitter lessons from experience.

This method can only be used rightly by those whose nature is purified, equilibrated, and stabilised, and who have risen above the baser aspects of life and the limitations of selfishness sufficiently to see life steadily and see it whole, and to realise that they are part of that larger whole and cannot separate themselves from it. The consequences of using this method wrongly are the same as the consequences of driving a car badly - the higher the power, the bigger the smash. The consequences of using it rightly are to obtain results quickly and effectually. The truly dedicated man never uses it for his own ends, or to further ambition, but always in relation to spiritual values. He says, "Not my will, but Thine be done"; surrenders himself unreserved to cosmic law, and invokes the One and Supreme Good at the commencement of each operation.

Having made his dedication and preparation, and accepted the responsibility for what he is about to do, he then proceeds to assemble the symbols associated with the sphere in which he proposes to work. Some he will make with his hands; some he will make with his imagination in the sphere of mind; but above all, he must be deeply imbued with the spiritual significance of the operation he proposes to perform.

This assembling of the symbols and formulating of the images has a two-fold function to perform; firstly, it induces long continued concentration; and secondly, it builds up the channels that shall serve to conduct the chosen force and puts the operator in touch with the source of this force. I have already given the principles involved in each stage and aspect of the operation, and the reader must bear these in mind in relation to the explanations being given in the present pages.

The operator uses the symbolic objects he has assembled as a means of inducing prolonged and profound concentration and stimulating his imagination; their function is to aid his mind-work; it is by means of the mind-work that the actual magic is done. It is in the plane of consciousness, the astro-mental plane, that results are experienced; and from this plane that they are realised in the ordinary way - by the actions and reactions of living creatures, so that they become manifest on the plane of form. It is the changing and energising of the mind of the operator that is the end aimed at in magic, and the result obtained. The mind, thus energised, becomes endowed with greatly extended powers, among which are clairvoyance, and telepathy of a type quite unrealised by the uninitiated, and the capacity to get into touch with cosmic forces which further reinforce its energies.

Chapter 7b

FOCUSING THE MAGIC MIRROR
Gareth Knight

Focusing the magic mirror is what in other terms might be called the tuning of consciousness, and it is done by concentrating the mind upon specific symbolic images.

There are very many of these and the earlier part of esoteric training lies in learning how to identify and to work with them. This comprises the basic five finger exercises of occult meditation. As someone learning to play the piano needs to know their scales, and to play them with facility, so does the magical apprentice need to learn the various scales of symbolic correspondences.

In their totality these are of infinite variety. For instance the esoteric symbolism of the East is different from that of the West; and different cultures throughout the world have their own pantheons of gods, their own body of legend and mythology. At first sight, this whole panoply may look like a vast confusion, as when, for instance, we scan the pages of an encyclopaedia of world mythology. But beneath the surface differences there is a common core, a bed rock of similarity, which is the common heritage of the human race as a whole.

If we are universally minded, we may try to integrate and synthesise a number of these systems by plunging into comparative mythology, and a fascinating exercise this can be. It is largely impractical though, just as it would be impractical for a musician to try to play every musical instrument in every possible style and genre. By the very nature of things we have to be selective, but this still leaves plenty of room for variety of expression.

We will find that there are sets of symbolism that make up into what we might call cosmic maps. That is to say, a whole complex of symbols held together in a patterned system of relationships. These will vary in style and detail but each will be an attempt to provide a model of the universe. And this also means a model of the human soul; for one of the axioms of esoteric philosophy is that the *microcosm* (that is to say the human being) is built to the same pattern as the *Macrocosm* (the universe at large).

One of the most familiar of esoteric symbol systems is the Tarot. It consists of a pack of 78 cards upon which are depicted a series of symbolic images. This readily breaks down into a pattern of four different suits numbered 1 to 10 together with four court cards. Beyond this four-fold pattern there exist 22 Trump cards, each representing a different archetype. A whole esoteric philosophy can be gleaned from meditating upon these images and the patterns they form.

Because of its universal application it can be used in different ways: in terms of ritual and directed visualisation, as I have described in my book *Tarot and Magic* (originally entitled *The Treasurehouse of Images*); or in the self instructional meditation and divination system I have demonstrated in *The Magical World of the Tarot*.

There are also other systems. The most comprehensive perhaps is the Tree of Life of the Qabalah, which is capable of relating a vast range of esoteric images including Tarot, astrology and the deep lore of the Hebrew number and letter system. It is also capable of throwing light on relationships between different god forms in various mythological systems. Small wonder then that it acts virtually as the back bone of the western esoteric tradition, with various text books on it including *The Mystical Qabalah* by Dion Fortune, and my own

A Practical Guide to Qabalistic Symbolism which also owes much to Dion Fortune and her school.

The Tree of Life, so very simple in its basic principles, is a network of triangles showing how inner forces inter-relate up and down the planes. It is thus capable of carrying a vast amount of symbolism, and making it readily available and comprehensible. It makes an ideal cosmic map when considered as a whole.

What is even more helpful is that it structures and subdivides the cosmos in a way that makes it more immediately and easily accessible. That is to say, that it is not only like an aerial photograph taken from such a height that one can see the city as a whole, but it is also sufficiently detailed to serve as a street map! That is to say, it has ten principle nodal points or spheres of influence which are joined by twenty-two paths, and a sound system of training can be based upon treading these paths in turn.

Although there is a set formal tradition about the images and symbols that may be met with upon each path, this structure can be amplified and modified by much ancillary symbolism and an important part of the training is not just to learn off by heart the traditional symbols but to develop the ability to discern with accuracy any related symbolism. Symbolism that is not necessarily published in books, that may be thrown up into consciousness when one treads each path at various levels.

There are various basic forms in which magical symbolism can be met, and the first obvious divide is between animate and inanimate images.

Inanimate imagery can first of all be regarded as the type of landscape through which we may pass on a visionary journey. Are we climbing a mountain? Following an ancient track over rolling hills? Going through a forest? On board a ship crossing the ocean? Or on a boat passing across a lake or along a river? Are we entering a cave or descending a tunnel into the earth? Are we under the sea? Are we flying?

If so, above the earth, or among strange planets, or in space between the stars? Do we seem to be in another time? Is it spring, summer, autumn or winter? Is it light or dark?

In all or any of these scenarios we have a different symbolic ambience. And one as wide and far ranging as may be met with in the whole of human imagination and human physical experience. It is the stuff of any human story, in fact or fiction or fantasy. Indeed story is the basic element in all of this. It is a form of the ultimate Quest. The search for who we are, from whence we come, and where we are going.

Passing from the landscape or the background of our journey, what symbolic place is it that we are making for? Is it a temple? A castle? A stone circle? A church? A hermit's hut? A tower? Even if found in the middle of a city it is likely to be a building of some kind.

And once within the building, what kind of room will we find ourselves in? A great hall? A dungeon? A chapel? A shrine? A meeting place?

And what is to be found there? An altar? A table? A window? And are there any objects to be seen on it or through it? A cup? A sword? A wand? A gem? A crown? The possibilities are endless - and all this is just in the realm of the inanimate.

When we turn to animate symbols we find that the power of our working may considerably increase. Are we seeing humans, or animals, or some other type of being?

If human are we meeting up with historical characters, with famous characters of fiction, with old friends, with relatives, with strangers, living or dead? Are they offering something or are they seeking something from us? Is it power, love, teaching, healing, the exchange of tokens or gifts? Here we have in potential the whole range of spirit guides at one level, or of "ascended masters" at another.

If they are not in human form? Well there is a whole range of animals, birds, fish, mythical beasts - even unicorns and dragons - some of which may be met with in the form of totem animals that will be like lucky mascots for us, or which may guide us further on our way, or have some heraldic or symbolic significance to demonstrate.

What of animate forms that are beyond those found in the natural forms of physical nature? The whole tradition of faery folk, be they sylphs, undines, salamanders, pixies, elves, hob goblins or whatever. From "lordly ones of the hollow hills" of the ilk of the Fairy King or Fairy Queen, powerful beings who in tradition can take human beings to another world where another form of time exists. It includes too the various ladies of the lake of Arthurian tradition. And all the way down to the gossamer fancies of the nursery. And also indeed the giants.

There is also the whole great and ancient tradition of the angels and various angelic beings, from the personal guardian angels that look after the destiny of individual human souls, to the principalities and powers that govern the destiny of nations, and ideas in the affairs of men and the rise and fall of cultures and civilisations, or the mighty beings all fire and devotion that cluster about the throne of God, the strange forms seen in vision by Ezekiel, and of course the more familiar archangels known by name as Gabriel, Michael or Raphael with particular vocations for bringing divine messages, giving protection, or healing. In more modern imaginative forms we may meet up with beings that might have come from science fiction stories.

So we find that we have a whole interior imaginative universe to explore, a veritable treasure house of images. But the fundamental question in our working with all or any of these images is how far do they represent our own imaginative projections and how far do they represent a reality of their own.

There is seldom likely to be a cut and dried answer to this, and only experience will bring anything approaching certainty. The poet Coleridge likened the situation to looking down into the waters of a well which has weeds growing upon the sides, some above the water and some below. It is very difficult to distinguish, when one looks into the waters, between weeds which are actually growing under the water and the reflections of weeds which are actually growing above. We have a similar situation in the assessment of the reality of magical experience.

That is really what we mean when we talk about the ability to focus our magic mirror. And also why the only valid criterion is the wisdom brought about by sustained practical experience.

Chapter 8a

CHANNELLING THE FORCES
Dion Fortune

Ceremonial rites are of varying degrees of efficacy. There are those, like the blameless and innocuous revels of the Buffaloes, which are incapable of bringing through any power of any sort; there are those like the Masons, which are usually inert, but are capable of power in the right hands; there are those like the Lord's Supper, which are never totally inert. The efficacy of a rite depends upon whether it is "contacted" or not. The ritual is simply a piece of psychological machinery; and just as a machine is designed to employ coal or petrol as a source of power, so rituals are designed to develop one or another type of spiritual energy. The principle of the transmission of power by means of gears remains constant, however, in every type of machine; and equally in rituals, the principle of the psychological technique for the exaltation of consciousness remains the same.

It only requires a very small amount of psychism to know whether a lodge is "on its contacts" or not: whether an adept is working with power or not. These things fluctuate considerably, both as to quantity and quality, and are never twice alike. The same familiar ceremony is not, therefore, boring to those who know what to look for, for one never quite knows what it is going to produce, within certain broad limits, in the way of inner experience.

The result of being "on a contact" is very marked. It is exactly like putting an engine in gear. There awakes in the soul a tremendous sense of dynamism and driving-power. The reason for this lies in the fact that by means of the appeal to the imagination of the symbolism of the ceremony, consciousness and subconsciousness are brought into alignment; there is a straight run-through of energy; the elemental dynamism of our nature is set free from the primitive levels of the mind, and at the same time is directed by the image held in consciousness by the imagination concentrating on the given symbol.

These symbols affect the subconscious mind in this manner because they are images belonging to the most ancient racial life. By their means consciousness and subconsciousness are united. It is a kind of tabloid psychoanalysis. The same results that the psychologist obtains by the prolonged and painful analysis of the dream-images are obtained quickly, effectually, and with a controlled reaction, by the occultist who knows the symbols to which the subconsciousness is conditioned by its racial heritage.

But although the release of subconscious energy explains a very great deal, it does not explain everything. The initiate simply regards it as a self-starter, and just as the motorist would not expect to run the car off the battery, so the initiate does not expect to achieve his ends simply by the use of his own subjective energy, though it is the release of this energy which enables him to pick up the corresponding cosmic force which is his objective.

This brings us to the consideration of the nature of these cosmic forces which form the objective of the practical occultist, and which, according to the traditional terminology he aims at "evoking to visible appearance". For the understanding of the nature of these forces we must refer to first principles, setting aside the practical approach we have pursued hitherto. In order to be brief I must be dogmatic, referring the reader for a fuller exposition of the subject to other of my books, notably, *The*

Mystical Qabalah which explains the methods employed by metaphilosophy in its researches.

Metaphilosophy conceives of the manifested universe as being emanated from what it calls the Great Unmanifest, which is beyond our conception as finite beings adapted to life on the planes of form. It does not, therefore, attempt to explain or define this source of all manifestation, but conceives of it by means of the symbol of an ever-welling fountain from which primal force rushes forth under pressure. This channel of becoming it calls the First Manifest, or God. The Unmanifest itself it conceives of under the symbol of interstellar space. There was a time when science declared the material universe to be a fixed system of energy, and gave a categorical denial to the doctrine I have outlined above; but nowadays it has come to the opinion that the sun receives energy from some point in outer space, so the esoteric concepts are no longer as alien to accredited opinions as they once were.

The esotericist conceives of this primal force as evolving through successive phases; developing special characteristics at each phase, establishing that particular mode of manifestation in existence, and then proceeding to overflow from it and evolve a further phase; the previous phase, however, still retaining its place in the scheme of things, just as the vertebrates evolved from the invertebrates, and then continued to exist side by side with their ancestral types. In esoteric terminology this is called the doctrine of emanations, and as Richard Payne Knight points out, it is found in all the ancient mythologies, eastern and western.

Each phase of manifestation, being established, continues to evolve in its own way, thus giving rise to contending stresses in the cosmos, which gradually achieve synthesis and equilibrium; giving rise, likewise, to the infinite diversity of manifesting life. These forces, primarily spiritual, pass through a phase of development analogous to consciousness of a very primitive type, and so on into manifestation in form, whether that form be a planet, a genus of plants or animals, or a race of human souls. Whatever has an organised form is organised about a spiritual nucleus, says the esotericist; and this form is the outward and visible sign of an inward and spiritual force evolving through experience.

This is a concept as widely removed from the accepted scientific doctrines as was the idea of an ever-becoming First Cause from the doctrine of a closed system of physical energy. Science, however, has bridged the gap in one case, so there is a possibility that it may do so in the other, and the esotericist, having seen science get across one ditch, is unwilling to be called a fool for biding his time to see if it will get across the other. Meanwhile, though unwilling to dogmatise in a matter which he cannot in the very nature of things hope to prove objectively, he takes his concept as a working hypothesis and bases it on a method which is traditionally called magic.

Let us now return from our digression to the consideration of magic as such. Granted that there are these different types of manifestation of primal energy, is it possible in any way to dissect them out and obtain them in a pure state at will? If this could be done, it would be an exceedingly valuable contribution to the world of applied science, even if it were arrived at purely empirically. One could, for instance, pick out a particular type of spiritual force, concentrate it, and apply it to remedy a deficiency or check an overplus of its opposite after the manner of a medicine.

This is what the occultist tries to do, and this is how he does it. He says that were it possible to contact any aspect of this evolving cosmic force in one of its primary phases, and to construct a channel for it to come down through the successive levels of evolving manifestation without getting diffused or confused with them, it would be possible to obtain it in a pure state, free and active. Now how is this to be done? He returns to his first position, that all force is primarily spiritual, evolving into consciousness and then into form, and presumes that the spiritual force he is trying to contact has in it the capacity to be reduced to a mental form. He says that it is reduced to that form when a mind conceives it, just as inorganic matter becomes organic when a living creature assimilates it; and as the building up of the inorganic into the organic is a function of life, so the conceiving of abstract spiritual force under a concrete mental form is a function of a super-consciousness, which bears the same relationship to subconsciousness that subconsciousness bears to consciousness.

By means of this abstract apprehension, then, it is possible, granted the necessary capacity in the individual, to come into touch with primary spiritual energy. Admittedly the untrained, uninstructed man will not achieve very much in these high fields, but granted the possibility of the trained and instructed man achieving something therein, what then is the next move?

Let it be remembered that this method was worked out during a very primitive phase of man's history, and has come down to us traditionally, and it bears the marks of its origin. These marks have obscured its value in the eyes of many at the present time, and made it the prey of the credulous, who alone were prepared to accept it without requiring it to change its spots. Spots, however, are only skin deep, and below the surface markings lies something fundamentally sound and useful, and this will become apparent when its archaic expression is restated in terms of modern thought (which restatement is my sole original contribution to the subject).

Primitive man, uninstructed by science, anthropomorphised, and concluded that intelligences similar to his own were behind natural phenomena. Now he would not have been very far out if he had said that life is more akin in its nature to mind than matter, and that the difference between animate and inanimate is in degree and not in kind; but he had not arrived at the point when he could conceive an abstract principle, and could only reason from the known to the unknown by very short removes; nevertheless, limited as were his resources, he succeeded in building up a very remarkable system which he called magic, but which subsequent generations would be doing no violence to terms if they called applied meta-psychology.

Putting aside the primitive philosophy of primitive man, let us examine his method. He personalised the forces behind the manifold appearances of the manifested universe, and concentrated his attention on these personifications by means of ritual. Did he obtain any results by so doing? That is exceedingly difficult to prove; the more important rites were done behind closed doors by initiates only, and everything that priestcraft and statecraft could do was done to conceal the reality and impress the populace. Truth, therefore, is hard to come by, and the real facts concerning the results obtained by the ancients will never be known.

There is sufficient data available, however, to enable us to repeat their experiments, and that is what the modern occultist is engaged in doing; the results he obtains are exceedingly interesting and instructive, and yield information about the mind, especially the unconscious mind, which could be of the greatest value in the right hands. Unfortunately it seldom comes into hands that can make it available, being collected under the conditions of occult secrecy which I have already deplored.

But although I have no hope that any words of mine will induce the generous pooling of resources which could be so valuable, I can at least offer my own observations and experiences for what they are worth.

It is not easy to find the right operators for an experiment with the traditional techniques. The credulous and the incredulous both falsify the results. Neither the credulity of a Bishop Leadbeater nor the incredulity of a Harry (Billygoat) Price are going to yield anything useful, because both start out with fixed ideas which would yield to nothing short of blasting-powder. For myself, I came to occultism with practical experience of psychoanalysis behind me, and I knew that the human mind had possibilities that were but little realised. I was not, therefore, incredulous of marvels as such, though I was decidedly sceptical of the explanations that were offered me. Putting aside the explanations I tried out the technique and found I got results. That was good enough for me. I knew that I was on the track of some form of reality; what it was, I did not know; but I was confident that if I worked at it boldly, and became expert in the rule of thumb technique I was being taught, I should get further insight into the nature of the forces with which we were operating and the phenomena we were producing. My position, therefore, might be described as one of devotional agnosticism.

This, I believe, is the right one for the experimenter. Let us accept the possibility of an invisible reality behind appearances; give the ancients credit for a system which was empirically sound, and try to find the conditions under which it can be made to work - rather than try to make it work under modern experimental conditions. Once experience and expertness are achieved, the conditions can be tightened up.

Chapter 8b

CHANNELLING THE FORCES
Gareth Knight

Ritual magical working is essentially a matter of handling polarities and this is why the symbolism of two pillars of contrasting colours appears so frequently in magical diagrams. A more dynamic way of representing this is in the Caduceus of Mercury, which shows two snakes coiling up a central wand giving a counterchange of colours at each level.

Polarity is of course a universal phenomenon, not only in the natural world but in the field of human relationships. Every conversational interchange, be it simply buying a postage stamp, has its polar aspect and the positive/negative aspects of this personal interchange are constantly free flowing and ever changing. Indeed if one unit in the equation were to be positive all the time and the other negative then we would have a very unusual and probably unhealthy situation indeed. The complete domination of one person by another, or of one group by another, is the mechanics of tyranny.

One may have certain reservations about hypnosis as well, in this respect, where the will of the entranced is in a highly negative state in relation to the suggestions of the hypnotist, although such situations may have a justification in therapy.

Very often circumstances in ordinary life lead to highly polarised situations. A commonplace example is a nervous car passenger who, feeling completely passive and at the mercy of the driver, seeks to restore the polar balance by being a very positive "back-seat driver".

Sexual dynamics tend to spring to mind at the mention of human polarities but though they may be very strong, they form but a part of the very wide spectrum of modes of human relationship. Freud may have seen the sexual drive at the back of most human activity but other psychologists, such as Adler or Jung, felt they could put equal importance on the drives for power or psychic integration. But whatever labels we seek to apply, most of our lives are taken up with polar interchange of one kind or another, whether in work or play, in close relationship or chance acquaintance.

Magical polarities in ritual are simply another mode of these general human principles and of no particular relevance to sexual relationships. Although as powerful dynamics are used in magical work, it follows that practitioners will prefer to avoid working with those who are looking to magic as compensation for some lack in their lives, be it in terms of sex, prestige, or other social deficiency.

Tantrik yoga is an eastern system of spiritual development that utilises sexual union in a highly disciplined form, but where the demands of self control exceed in rigour anything likely to be found in regimes where the ideals are those of chastity. Attempts at western practice of the art suffer similar problems that pertain to adapting other advanced forms of yoga, and may well end up as an esoteric cloak for sexual adventure seasoned with hypocrisy. All too often, when sex comes in the door of the lodge, any worthwhile magic flies out of the window.

Magical polarities are of two kinds - usually called horizontal and vertical. The horizontal polarity is that which goes, so to speak, across the floor of the lodge. Vertical polarity is an inner relationship between a lodge officer and an inner plane source of power. This is a priestly or mediating role.

In practice, the two forms of polarity work together. An officer gets on his or her "contacts" (a vertical polarity) and then mediates the power of that contact into the lodge (a horizontal polarity).

There are thus within this operation two skills that need to be cultivated. The ritual officer should have a foot in each of two worlds, and act as a link between them. Failure to work efficiently in either is to fail in the work as a whole.

Thus we have the two poles, when taken to extremes, of how *not* to work a ritual office. An officer who operates only vertically may well have wonderful personal realisations but will not be of much help to the work of the lodge as a whole. While an officer who operates only horizontally is simply putting up a facade. This might perhaps fool or even impress an inexperienced onlooker but will plainly be a sham to anyone of psychic sensitivity. There is a lot more to ritual technique than graceful movement, good voice production and projection, or even an imposing presence. Yet the absence of these is a dire disadvantage in ritual however powerful the individual's inner contacts.

Traditionally ritual magicians learn their skills by the apprenticeship system. They sit in upon the work of their more experienced journeymen or master craftsmen and gradually are accorded greater responsibility according to their developing abilities. It has to be said, however, that as with many skills in life, some may be more adept at ritual performance than others, irrespective of their innate spiritual worth or condition. Much the same kind of thing applies in any other performance related art . It can happen though that some, although not gifted ritually, may be very perceptive of inner conditions and thus can play a very useful role in reporting their psychic impressions of a working.

One of the difficulties and skills of being a ritual officer is having to function on more than one plane at once. Coping with scripts and ritual actions of one kind and another is without doubt a distraction from sustained inner plane awareness and mediation of subtle forces. It follows that anyone who attends a ritual *without* the responsibility of taking office has a better chance of appreciating all that is going on. This is not to deny that, for the officers concerned, there is a great thrill and sense of satisfaction in being able to mediate a hefty ritual office on full bore.

Another type of valuable lodge member, who may not necessarily be well gifted at ritual performance, is the "catalyst". The term is borrowed from chemistry where it signifies an element or compound whose presence is necessary for a chemical reaction to take place but which apparently seems to take no active part itself. There are also people like this, who sometimes feel frustrated about their seeming lack of psychic or ritual ability, yet about whom things seem to happen the more easily. This is no doubt because the human being is a very complex psychic and spiritual organism indeed, and like an iceberg, all our gifts and latent powers may not be apparent when viewed above the surface level of physical perception. In such a case the vertical and horizontal polarities are working at an unconscious level.

In the classic type of ritual set-up as exemplified in published Masonic rites, the horizontal polarity of the lodge works initially in an east-west direction, the magus or chief officer of the lodge being seated in the east and the next senior being directly opposite, in the west. The magus is in some respects like a faucet situated midway between inner and outer planes, between the assembled lodge upon the physical plane, and the assembled spiritual beings associated with the lodge upon the inner planes. And while this mediating function is part and parcel of every lodge officer, and indeed of every person present, its main thrust and burden falls upon the eastern officer, who may have to carry the brunt of any unbalanced force if for any reason the lodge is not working in an equilibrated way.

The power thus comes from the east, the direction of greatest symbolic light, and moves like the sun toward the west. From here, in the normal course of events it will circulate round to the southern office and then be distributed to the rest of the lodge either directly or via the northern office. This is the functioning of horizontal polarity as magically understood. The source of the power however lies on the inner levels, which is tapped by means of vertical polarity. There are many variants to this basic pattern that are beyond our present scope but what we cite may serve as a general guide for channelling the forces involved in ritual.

These forces may then be directed beyond the lodge to the world at large, which can also be done in various ways. In essence the whole ritual is a form for channelling or preserving powers made available by spiritual beings upon the inner planes who have been contacted by the work in hand.

An example of this is the evocation of the Chapels of Remembrance which we have already cited. Here we have the formation of a particular imaginative complex upon the inner planes which may remain in being for use over a considerable period of time. It remains in form and function, rather like an astral satellite, for those upon the inner or the outer planes who have need of it.

The action of vertical polarity may also bring about the manifestation of what are sometimes called "signs following". That is to say coincidental happenings upon the physical plane that are related to the inner plane work in hand. To some extent there is a subjective side to this. Anyone who has been an expectant mother or father knows the phenomenon that suddenly the streets seem full of pregnant women. There are of course no more than there always were, it is simply that now they are being consciously noticed, through the sympathy of shared experience.

An example of this in a magical context might be that on the way home from a ritual concerning Robin Hood one is struck by the sign of a public house called "The Sherwood Forester", not noticed before, despite passing it many times. Needless to say it was always there, but it comes into conscious recognition, not by coincidence or as a genuine following sign, but simply because by virtue of the recent work the mind is magically tuned to it.

This is the subjective element of signs following but there can also be an objective side, an example of which is the way that various First World War related objects came the way of the initiate bringing through the Chapel of Remembrance imagery. This involved being closely in touch with an inner plane contact who was working through the personality of a British officer of the First World War who had allegedly been killed at Ypres. And one of the objects that came her way was an old picture postcard of Ypres of the period.

*S: May I ask you an awkward question? How **did** you get that postcard to me?*

M: Aha! Now that would be giving away an Inner Plane Adeptus trade secret. But just so you don't think I'm trying to wriggle out of the question I will endeavour to explain a bit about how it works. As often as not it's a simple case of leading you to discover something that's already there, by dropping the relevant directions into your subconscious. That - to all intents and purposes - is how you happened upon that big bucket of poppies the other day when you went out to buy lamp oil. You were only buying the lamp oil in the first place because your supplies had been depleted by your candle-lit conversations with me, so that was an easy one to steer you into. The Ypres postcard was a little more tricky, and the fact that it is now acting as a strong talismanic link, powerfully charged with a sense of my presence, is an indication of the level of effort required from me to put it in your possession. It is extremely difficult for us here to effect changes on the outer plane without the aid of mediators such as yourself, and it necessitates a great deal of force from this end, with no guarantee that it is going to work anyway. All we can do from here is project our own wills with as much gusto as possible and rely on the natural tides of psychic force to carry out the action. It's not unlike sending a message in a bottle - you have to throw it out to sea with substantial force to get it far enough away to be picked up by the tide, and you can never be sure whether it's going to go the right way. So I am as pleased as you are that the postcard turned up, and if you think *yourself hard done by that you had to fork out twenty pence to purchase it, just bear in mind how much effort it cost me! I think you got the bargain end of the deal. No doubt you are thinking though that it is a bit of a rummy coincidence that a card from Ypres of all places should turn up among a handful of bits of old junk in a bookshop, and that there must be more to it than my simply steering your subconscious mind towards it. Indeed there is. Various conjunctions of circumstances have come together, possibly over many years, to enable that card to be for sale in a bookshop in which you will be able to find it at the appropriate time. It is indeed possible (note that I say possible, not probable, nor certain) that the card was destined for you from the moment it was first purchased, and has spent the last eighty years or so finding its way from Belgium to England and gradually working its way towards that particular bookshop on the tides of destiny, to enable it to be collected by you at the moment when your fate conjoins with the card's fate. This may seem quite preposterous, the idea of your destiny being linked with the destiny of a picture postcard, to the extent that it is on its way to you half a century before your birth, especially bearing in mind that this conjunction of destinies has been instigated by me - which seems to imply that I was aware of you fifty odd years before your birth and was also aware that you would make conscious contact with me twenty-seven years into your incarnation and that you would frequent a particular bookshop at this time. Rather an unlikely contingency! But it's actually quite simple when you bear in mind (if you can) that time as a linear concept is an illusion innate within human consciousness. Obviously there is nothing I can do to induce an understanding of time as it exists on the inner planes, since your consciousness is programmed to perceive it as a rigidly linear concept. Suffice to say that I am not bound by such time restrictions, or should I say not **the same** time restrictions, and that is how I **appear** to make things happen retrospectively. It is important to note that it is a mere **appearance**, and that I am not **actually** manipulating your past - that is simply how it will seem to you in your human perspective. Thus I can attempt to set a chain of linked circumstances to knock each other along (like knocking over a* *line of up-ended domino pieces) to enable that card to be in that shop at the moment in time that you call 2nd March 1996 (although all that, as you know, is a useful but meaningless intellectualisation, since time is far too abstract to be thus measured and labelled), but it will seem to you in your 'linear time' perspective that all those circumstances have already happened, and are 'in the past', whereas in the cosmic scale of time (scale being a misnomer, because as I said, time does not lend itself well to being quantified) these events may be effectively simultaneous, or in a different order altogether. This is a vastly complex subject, and I fear that I have done little to elucidate it. Rather, I am bombarding you with concepts that you are not equipped to comprehend. But it is quite interesting to see how far I can push these ideas in your human intelligence - I don't see how incarnate souls can be expected to evolve unless they are pushed a little beyond their natural boundaries every now and then.*

And later:

M: *I would like to start by adding a few comments to our last topic of conversation, concerning the way in which Inner Plane Adepti can induce some of these odd little coincidences that liven up your outer plane work. As I said, we can have no direct controlled effect upon the physical plane, for the simple reason that we don't have bodies (a small price to pay for such freedom, I must say!) and we rely on the ambient tides of force to carry our intentions into actuality. This has probably given you the impression that it's rather a hit and miss affair. And so it is, but not so much as you might think. There is a cosmic law to the effect that these tides of force (the forces responsible for the general trends in outer plane experience, the tendencies and the coincidences) are attracted to that grey area of merged consciousness which I once referred to as No Man's Land. Or perhaps it's the other way around, and our merged consciousnesses are attracted to the tides of force which abound on the physical plane. Anyway, it's that vortex produced by our mutual thoughts, our conjoined consciousness, that does the biz. Thus I could think about a particular item or concept until I'm blue in the face (so to speak) and nothing would happen, and you could think about that same item or concept until you're blue in the face too, and nothing would happen. But if we overlap our thoughts so that I am conscious of your consciousness and you are conscious of my consciousness (which is exactly what's happening now) then our mutual concentration sets up a kind of energised imprint which straddles the planes (I'm really struggling to get this into words without misleading you) and this acts as a kind of cosmic magnet, so that as those force tides flow over and around it they are pulled in towards it. There, you* **do** *understand, and I'm very pleased. Thus our conjoined consciousness has been focused on the sacrifices of the Great War, and this (although you may well not have been aware of it) created an energised imprint linking the inner and outer planes. And then along came the forces (on my plane, I should add, as well as on yours) which were immediately drawn in towards our imprint, as if to a magnet, and caused the forces to flow in that direction - hence the sudden spate of coincidences. Of course, these forces cannot over-ride your free will, so they can't necessarily make things happen to you, but they do create a certain tendency for any objects linked with the Great War to gravitate towards you. Compree? These poppies and wartime postcards and photographs and such like are as steel pins to the magnet of your energised consciousness. So it* **is** *really just a coincidence that you keep finding things in the physical world which seem to link up with whatever you've been meditating on recently, but it is* **induced** *coincidence if you like, a kind of side effect of the work you are doing. So you see it was me that made you find that Ypres postcard, but not through direct control - rather through a fortunate coincidence. No doubt you are wondering whether similar things are happening to me on the inner plane. Well, it's all a bit different here, and our little vortex on the Great War isn't causing me to see poppies everywhere, but it is having a real and very positive effect. Meaningful coincidences are really an outer plane phenomenon, and very positive in their own way. There's nothing better for concentrating the* **mind, and they help to reassure you that you are properly linked up and on the right track. I have of course been talking about this on a pretty simplistic level. But the same principle does apply to high-powered group ritual magic. If the mere tuning in of your mind to my mind and vice versa is sufficient to spark** *off all those interesting coincidences, just think how big and powerful an imprint is produced when there are ten or twelve trained minds sitting in a circle linked up to the trained minds of the Inner Plane Adepti and any other inner plane contacts which are working within the group. All that lot, energised by meditation, ritual intention, and invoked forces, consolidates into a whopper of a magnet. The effect of such high-powered working on the ether of both inner and outer plane is pretty formidable, and the forces which are drawn in towards it can bring about some powerful and very positive effects. That's magic!*

Chapter 9a

THE FORM OF THE CEREMONY
Dion Fortune

Let us next consider what are the criteria by which we are to judge whatever results, or lack of them, may be obtained. Are we to look for phenomena manifesting upon the physical plane? Under certain conditions, I think we can; the condition being that a materialising medium is present. When I first began to work along these lines there was quite a lot of incidental phenomena in the shape of raps and bangs and a curious sound as if a cracked wine glass were being struck with a knife blade; balls of light rolled about in an aimless fashion; we heard bell-like notes and voices calling the names of those present, and on one occasion a door panel split right across when a banishing ritual was being done. I made no attempt to produce such phenomena; I did not expect them, and I had no control over them. I noticed, however, that they always appeared when I was feeling depleted and nervy, a condition of which I saw a great deal in those days, and the worse I felt, the more marked were the phenomena. Some years later an occult operation was performed that sealed up my aura, and I have had no more of the exhaustion and no more of the phenomena save on rare occasions when I have been in occult difficulties; I have had occasional slight returns of the depletion, and with it, of the phenomena, the two coming and going together. Therefore, I conclude they are associated together. If physical phenomena are produced by the erudition of ectoplasm, whatever that may be, from a materialising medium, the coincidence of my exhaustion and my phenomena would be explained. None of my work has ever been done under test conditions; in one way this is unfortunate, for nothing can be conclusively proved by it; but in another way it has been fortunate, for I have obtained a range of experience which I think would have been nipped in the bud by more exactness in the early stages.

There is unquestionably a great deal to be learnt from physical phenomena, and their bearing upon physiology and biology should be recognised. Here is a field for exact research where the methods of the laboratory are valuable. But it is by no means the whole sphere of operation, and when one leaves the tangible behind and passes over into the sphere of psychic experience, one passes out of the realm of physical science and enters upon psychology, and methods must change accordingly. Freud and Jung obtained their results by examining enormous quantities of mental material upon its own level, making no attempt to reduce it to the plane of dense matter, unless the word reaction tests of Jung can be conceived to do so. This, I believe, to be the right approach to magical phenomena. Let us examine the mental content of the experimenters and see what we find there, and how the contents classify when we have collected sufficient bulk to strike an average. If we expect to see the Devil appear in the Triangle of Art, complete with pitchfork and leaving behind cloven scorch marks on the carpet, we are barking up the wrong tree. A great Authority said "The Kingdom of Heaven is within you", and I have myself seen several very adequate private hells.

Ceremonial magic is not primarily designed to produce objective phenomena, but to operate in the invisible kingdoms. The immediate results are not observed by the physical eye, but by psychic vision, and the end results are diffused and indirect, but nevertheless very definite. If we approach ceremonial magic from this point of view, we can learn a great deal, and we can also do a great deal; but if we expect of it what it is not designed to perform, we shall be disappointed. The reason that so many magical experiments undertaken for research purposes prove abortive is that too much is expected and too little is done. Certain conditions have to be fulfilled; these are laid down very specifically in all the ancient rituals; the difficulty is to obtain moderns who will carry them out.

It must be clearly realised that magic can only be done effectually by a trained person, and that results are not a foregone conclusion, but in proportion to skill and experience. Natural aptitude also plays a part. The first requisite is the power to concentrate; the second, the power to build up an image in the imagination with the same clarity as a novelist visualises his characters; the third is the power to throw consciousness out of gear and let the subconscious mind "take over". These are all things which can be learnt by practice along the right lines. They take time, and they require work, but it can be done. It is also necessary to have a thorough knowledge of the cosmic principles outlined upon an earlier page. One then knows what types of force are available for contacting, and how, when and where they can be contacted; likewise whether the conditions are available for a specific operation.

The operator, and I am talking now about the initiated adept and not the rule of thumb dabbler in the psychic, next proceeds to gather together the instruments of the operation. Two rules are observed: first, that everything must be virgin, that is to say, it must never have been used for any other purpose; and secondly, that the more trouble it costs, the better. The reason for the first rule is that any sensitive can feel the influences that have been associated with an article he handles, and when one is doing ceremonial, one gets into a sensitive condition; as the most important point in magical workings is concentration, one does not wish to be distracted by alien influences. The how, why and wherefore of this fact I will not digress upon at present, but refer the reader to what I have already said concerning the power of the Astral Aether to take on forms.

Concerning the second point, that the more trouble one takes the better, the explanation is readily understood, for it comes within known territory. The trouble you take helps you to prolong your concentration. It is much easier to concentrate on your hazel wand while you are whittling at it than to concentrate upon it with your hands folded in your lap. It is the Froebel action song principle that we have noted before.

The whole ceremonial upon the physical plane is directed to this end, being expressly designed to assist concentration and exalt imagination. When, however, one knows the principle involved, it is not necessary to go to the enormous amount of expense and trouble suggested by various writers. The person trained in concentrating will put in half an hour's hard mental work and obtain the requisite result. As a matter of fact, the initiate in the course of his training works with the different cosmic factors and gains mastery of each in turn, so when he comes to the specific work of a magical experiment he has, as it were, the raw material ready to his hand and has merely to mould it into the requisite form. To the experienced operator no paraphernalia is necessary. He can sit in his chair and visualise the whole temple and ceremony and obtain as good, and even better results than are obtained by the actual rite; but when a team of operators are working together, as is usual in magical operations, it is essential to have a properly equipped temple and a set ceremony in order to co-ordinate their efforts. In fact, even for the solitary worker, it is a great help to go through the rite on the physical plane. It assists concentration and enhances the imagination.

The temple is equipped with the symbolic furniture in such a way that it appeals to the imagination and turns it in the desired direction. That is the real principle involved. But imaginations are of different types, and the imagination of the trained occultist has been "conditioned" by years of work and psychic experience, and each experience will be associated with a particular symbol, and it is to this "conditioning" that the equipment of a temple is designed to speak. That is why outsiders are never admitted, for they must be "conditioned" to a symbol before it will mean anything to them.

Next comes the choice of the team for the performance of the specific rite. They have to be chosen on type, granting of course, the necessary training. One would not invite an elderly and repressed spinster, given to good works, to assist at a rite of Pan. Ceremonies vary enormously in type, but let us take for example a ceremony of invocation. Now invocation and evocation are not the same thing. Evocation is what the spiritualists do when they get a departed soul to communicate; invocation calls down the primary spiritual forces.

It is a maxim in magic that all the gods are one god, and all the goddesses are one goddess, and there is one initiator; nevertheless, the gods and goddesses of the different pantheons and the archangels of the Qabalah represent different specialised aspects of force. The particular deity you elect to use as a channel of invocation is purely a matter of taste and expediency. Isis, Ceres, Aphrodite and the Archangel Haniel are all different notes in the same scale; they will not yield identical results, but they all represent different aspects of the same potency. The same temple and equipment will do for all of them.

For such a rite, according to tradition and experience, three persons are necessary, one to direct, control and steady the ceremony; one to bring through the power, and one to receive it. The first of the three must keep his wits about him; the other two should lose themselves in the ceremony. It is by the action and reaction between these two, as between two actors on a stage, that the atmosphere is worked up; the first operator might be likened to the producer.

The work starts by building up in the imagination of all concerned an imaginary temple, which is conceived of as covering and enclosing the physical temple. This is usually done by drawing signs in the air towards the four cardinal points and visualising a ring of light connecting them. This is conceived to form an astral barrier. Next the operators solemnly dedicate themselves to the power that is to be invoked. Then, if the method of assumption of god-forms is to be used, one of their number sets to work to imagine that he is the priest of that god and that the god is descending and taking possession of him; the others act accordingly. This, of course, is obviously the method of a medium going under control; the being invoked, however, is not a departed spirit, but a cosmic force deliberately personified under an imaginary but standard form.

The result of such an operation, if successful, is to produce a profound psychological effect on all concerned and an extraordinary atmosphere in the room where it is performed. If bungled, or used injudiciously, the results can, of course, be unpleasant; but used well and skilfully, the results have to be seen to be believed. They are capable of very wide practical applications, especially in the sphere of psychotherapy.

And what are these results? No-one but a psychic will see anything, for there is nothing physical to be seen; but people who normally are not psychic at all are often made temporarily psychic by the ceremony. No-one, I should think, could sit through a ceremony worked with power and not be affected by it, even if the effect produced is no more than exasperation. Those who are in sympathy with what is being done experience a very marked exaltation.

Now if temporary exaltation and nothing more were produced, ceremonial magic would rank with alcohol as an intoxicant with possible medicinal uses and a definite entertainment value; but such an exaltation extends consciousness, develops capacity, and affects character in a very marked degree. It will not change a person's character, making him something he is not, but it will bring out anything of a corresponding nature that is latent in just the same way that hypnotism will, and for the same reason - that it touches the deepest levels of consciousness and releases inhibitions. It is for this reason that ceremonial will do in an hour what can only be done by meditation in months or years. Being a very potent method, it has to be in skilled hands, but rightly used, it is exceedingly effective, and there is no reason whatever why it should be in any way harmful or dangerous.

The persons taking part must be carefully chosen, both for their own sakes and for the sake of the success of the operation; they must be properly trained and know what they are about, and they must gain experience with minor potencies and rites before they attempt the high-powered ones.

Some exponents of occultism decry all ritual as dangerous, and no doubt it would be so in their hands; but there is no reason why foxes who have got tails should cut them off. I have taken part in many hundreds of rituals, and I have upon occasion seen things go wrong and accidents happen; I consider that in untrustworthy or ignorant hands one has the makings of very serious trouble; I have had trouble with magic myself, and I have helped to pick up the pieces after other folks' trouble; I have never, however, seen a normal person take any permanent harm provided the appropriate occult remedies were promptly applied when things went wrong; but no ceremonial working ought to be attempted except under the direction of someone who knows what they are about and has had experience of this line of work, so that these remedies may be to hand when required. The only serious danger is to mentally unbalanced or neurotic persons, and a ceremony might be quite enough to push such a one over the borderline of insanity who otherwise would have managed to get along all right. It is for this reason that alienists say that spiritualism and occultism drive people insane. They will not drive normal people insane, but they soon prove too much for the unstable. On the other hand, however, the knowledge gained in practical occultism could be of extraordinary value in certain types of mental disease; those types, that is to say, that are diseases of the personality and not due to organic or toxic causes.

I maintain, therefore, that ceremonial operations justify themselves just as surgery justifies itself by obtaining quick and radical results; but I not only admit, but warn, that it is subject to the same risks as surgery - faulty judgement and faulty technique on the part of the operator, and bad risks among patients.

Chapter 9b

THE FORM OF THE CEREMONY
Gareth Knight

A ritual can take various forms according to the type of symbolism that is being worked with - be it Qabalistic, Greek, Egyptian, Christian, Celtic or whatever. However, the underlying structure will be very much the same, conforming to specific general laws, in much the same way that a room may be furnished in many different styles but fundamentally must comprise a sound floor, a sound ceiling, sound walls, at least one door and probably some windows, with provision for heating, lighting, ventilation and possibly running water.

In like manner, a ritual will consist of some form of opening, a statement of intention, contacting the forces concerned, channelling them to a particular aim or climax, and then a closing.

As to basic furniture, the minimum is probably a circle of chairs - unless the work is performed standing. However a central focus will be a common requirement, and this will usually be marked with a simple light or with an altar or central table upon which various symbols may be set. Raised daises or rather more ornate chairs at the quarters for the officers are an optional extra - the important factor being the efficiency of the officer who is sitting there, the practicality and comfort of the chair, rather than its symbolic or aesthetic lineaments. A beautifully carved ritual throne is more of a liability than an asset if it squeaks at the slightest movement, or tortures the incumbent with discomfort after fifteen minutes.

Other symbolic furniture such as pillars or floor cloths may be utilised but are the gilt upon the gingerbread. The basic purpose of such accoutrements is simply to direct the attention to the operators (inner and outer) to appropriate places in the lodge lay-out. It serves much the same basic purpose as white lines in the roadway for pedestrians and motorists. Similarly bells or knocks at appropriate places are aids to inner plane presences to key in to the different phases of a complex ritual, or to mark particularly important points.

One elementary mistake with beginners is to spend so much time and effort on an elaborate opening that energy levels and attention span have been considerably reduced by the time one gets to the main work of the lodge. There is no point in getting so stuffed up with *hors d'oeuvres* that one cannot do justice to the main meal.

The basic formula is for the magus, or senior officer, to circumambulate the lodge. That is, to walk round it three times intent upon focusing and concentrating some etheric force from the electro-magnetic aura of each one present. Then to make a statement of reverent dedication at each of the four quarters by means of a short verbal formula and some appropriate sign. This is at root a balancing up of the lodge, like a boat, upon the waters of the unseen.

Following this the magus should state the purpose of the rite. This is an important element in magic, however brief, as it formulates and focuses the combined spiritual will of those assembled. Then the magus makes formal contact with each of the lodge officers. This is generally done in a somewhat repetitive fashion by a series of formal questions and instructions to which the officer responds appropriately. "What is your situation in the lodge?" "Why so situated?" "What quality do you represent?" "What is its symbol?" "Then place that symbol upon the altar to signify that those powers are functioning in the lodge." When this is done, a salute may be exchanged between the officer and the magus. The whole intention is a steady build up of power and focused attention, affirming who is running the show, what its intention is, and sounding out the individual notes that go to make up the vibrating chord of the whole ritual.

The element of repetition is psychologically as well as magically effective in building up the framework of the ritual. The ultimate effectiveness of the rite will depend on the degree of vertical polarity that can be rendered available as horizontal polarity, as we have previously defined. This will be felt very forcibly by the officers concerned, very often with physiological sensations of heat, or at the head chakras increased heart beat, or prickling or itching sensations particularly

There will also be, in major rituals, a marked change in the atmosphere, which can be detected by sensitive persons, even if they are not actually present at the ritual but are within the same building or near vicinity. Anyone of a sceptical turn of mind, or otherwise out of sympathy with the work in hand, and perhaps not even realising their latent psychic faculties, may register the effect in some other way, often by a minor emotional upset, such as a feeling of irritability.

Physical phenomena are extremely rare, in or out of the lodge, to the point of being regarded more as pathologies than desiderata. They are only likely to occur when a particularly powerful personality has what might be termed a leaky aura, or of the type that in the spiritualist world is regarded as a "materialising medium". That is to say, giving off a raw kind of subtle energy at the boundaries of physical substance which can be manipulated by thought power.

Anyone of this fairly rare condition is likely to feel somewhat depleted as a result of this, but all present at a ritual contribute some degree of etheric magnetism to the work in hand, whether they realise it or not. For this reason any who are working on low energy levels or are nervously run down in any way, may tend to drop off to sleep in ritual conditions. This is a relatively harmless condition but is best avoided, as it indicates a temporary lack of control on the etheric levels, and alternately sagging and jerking heads and even light snores are not particularly contributive to the work of the lodge!

Other slight problems that sometimes occur with beginners at ritual is the stimulating of the psychic centre at the throat, which can lead to distracting fits of coughing. In such circumstances it is best for the person concerned to have a good cough and have done with it, as the growing sense of desperation and embarrassment in trying to suppress it is likely to be even more disruptive upon the subtler planes. Seasoned ritualists will not be distracted by coughs, sneezes or any of the thousand and one noises from the immediate environment. Indeed suppressing noise without an impractical degree of soundproofing is almost a physical impossibility in modern conditions. It is easier to learn to live with it and work through it.

When the opening has been fully completed, which should not take more than twenty minutes at the most, the main work of the day can commence. This may be a matter of moving symbolic objects about but is more likely to consist of directed visualisation. Even where physical ritual actions are performed, the accompanying inner visualisation is a highly important part of the process. This is where the skill comes in to ritual office - in working upon two levels at once. Remaining deeply on contact and in meditation without setting fire to oneself, spiking the ceiling with a ritual sword, spilling the chalice over your neighbour, and coping with the many things that can and may go wrong but which careful forethought and rehearsal should avoid.

Closing is another part of ritual work that is fraught with misunderstanding. This is largely a result of a fearful and credulous ambience that attaches to magic as a result of its treatment in fiction, and the antics of its lunatic fringe.

The principal purpose of a closing formula is not to do with keeping demons at bay. But when a ritual performance has tuned the consciousness of individuals to a particularly high level it is appropriate to close things down gently so that they can go and catch their buses or drive their cars without being a hazard to themselves or to others. However, if circumstances permit, as perhaps in a residential environment, and when the place of working is not immediately needed, then it can be beneficial not to close the rite down completely, but to let the beneficent forces continue to flow.

When a formal closing is used, it is generally similar to the opening, only in reverse. The object is to bring back the focus of consciousness to normal functioning upon the physical plane, which means that there is not likely to be quite the elaboration and evocatory charisma of the opening. The words may be rendered in almost a matter of fact but firm manner rather than chanted or intoned. The reverse circumambulations of the magus are intended to disperse any accretion of etheric force back to the members of the circle, a matter simply rendered by spiritual intention rather than any formulary, and then the members of the lodge disperse. In some circles the magus and officers may march out ceremonially and the rest be ushered out by a minor officer. In others members may simply leave quietly in their own time.

The ideal working place is a temple set apart from all mundane activities. This is rarely possible, but fortunately is not essential, and nor is the permanence, cost and elaboration of ritual furniture directly proportional to the effectiveness and power of ritual being performed. A good ritual group, even if it is working in uncongenial surroundings with transportable equipment will make its own atmosphere, its own power points in the inner ethers. Just as a good dance can be had by rolling back the carpet and pushing the furniture to the walls, so can a good ritual.

We have mentioned the general problem of noise and it is well to remember that this is a two way thing. The enthusiastic chanting of magical formulae, to say nothing of the smell of incense wafting into the outside world, is not likely to go without comment - or at least suspicion of dire goings on. However, as long as the incense does not smell too much like illegal substances there is not likely to be a police raid.

On the subject of incidental hazards to ritual however, it is reported that the New York Police Department do not take kindly to ritual swords being transported in public places, and this form of official nervousness could pertain elsewhere. Certainly I have been somewhat apprehensive in transporting hollow pillars past London Airport when the IRA was currently using drainpipes for mortar attacks. It is possible, of course, that ritual robes accompanying such ritual artefacts may persuade the authorities of one's non-violent intent.

Ritual robes are largely a matter of local custom. Certain pagan groups dispense with them, along with the rest of their clothing, altogether. Organised groups traditionally have a uniform set of robes or even cassocks. When it comes to expense and elaboration much the same criteria apply as to ritual location and furniture. A poor ritual performance is not likely to be much improved by gorgeous robes and a richly furnished temple. Whilst the experienced ritualist will be able to operate effectively in ordinary clothes in any environment.

However, there is a certain "magic" in dressing up, particularly if the robes have attained a certain ambience through exposure to incense on various occasions - which does not mean to say that they should not be washed when necessary! They will also carry an association of ideas, which is helpful to personal ritual preparation, and putting on robes can and should be a little private opening ritual in itself. Taking off the consciousness and preoccupations of the outer world with one's ordinary clothes, and putting on the elements of higher consciousness with one's magical robe, cloak, shoes, lamen, cord, head-dress or whatever is customarily used.

Chapter 10a

THE PURPOSE OF MAGIC
Dion Fortune

There are three schools of thought in regard to the occult arts. The first, which I will call the rationalistic, attributes them altogether to the power of the subconscious mind. The second attributes them wholly to supernatural agencies such as the intervention of the spirits of the departed, elementals, archangels, and *hoc genus omne*. This we will call the credulous school of occult thought. The third, of which I believe I am the founder, and of which I am at any rate a member, attributes the phenomena produced by means of the occult arts to the interaction of both factors, together with an intelligent practical application of certain esoteric knowledge concerning the nature of the universe. The viewpoint I would like to label the metaphysical school of occult thought.

First, then, let us recognise that all occult art, like all pictorial or musical art, must rest upon a basis of the natural and acquired skill of the artist - in the case of the occultist, the development of certain little-understood capacities latent in every mind in varying degrees, but totally absent in none, and comparable in this respect to the capacity for musical expression. Without this basis, the most powerful magical formula is like a violin in the hands of an orang-utan, to adapt Balzac's famous comment.

But however great the development of the human mind as such, it has its limitations, and it is here that the consideration of the supernatural begins. According to the occult hypothesis, matter is the end product of a long course of evolution involving phases of gradually increasing density and definiteness of organisation. We must look for the sources of matter in this subtle background of unembodied forces, and in their combinations and permutations for the root causes of the events that appear in the physical world and for which no satisfactory physical explanation is forthcoming, such as the appearance of life itself on this globe; the intrinsic nature of chemical and physical activity; birth, mating, death; disease and regeneration, not to mention all the processes dealt with by psychology, which by all save the die-hard materialist are regarded as primarily non-physical, though admittedly modified by physical influences.

Much of the subtle substance of this invisible realm as is organised in the form we are familiar with as dense matter, is held in firm bondage to the laws of the plane of matter and is very hard to detach therefrom. Nevertheless, the rigidity of the bonds varies in different forms of organisation, from the associations of electrons into those stable forms which chemistry calls the elements, to the exceedingly labile physiology of the neurotic. As every chemist knows, organic chemistry is one thing, and inorganic chemistry is another; and as every doctor ought to know, there is a very great difference between the stably organised physiological orchestra of a healthy agricultural labourer and that of a highly strung emotional actress. The more creative the intelligence, the more labile is the physiology.

This shows us that the greater the proportion of mind to matter, the greater the influence of mind over matter. The occultist carries his deduction a step further, and says: "Detach mind from matter and you have free-moving force; it is matter, and matter alone that imposes any degree of fixity upon mind." Now this is an important point in the occult hypothesis - the freedom of mind apart from matter, and the fixation of mind by means of matter. It should be carefully noted, for upon it the whole occult technique is based.

The first aim of an occultist is to learn to detach mind from matter, and having so detached it, then to control it by attaching it to chosen forms. If he can detach mind from matter, he can direct it as he will, but not otherwise, for the stimuli of the senses direct it for him. But unless he immediately re-attaches it to the plane of form, it will degenerate into formless force that like the wind that bloweth where it listeth, and he heareth the sound therof, but that is about all. In actual practice therefore, he does not risk allowing thought to escape from his control, but detaches it from matter - that is to say, attention to the objects of sense - by attaching it to objects that do not belong to the world of sense though derived therefrom. In other words, the reflections in his imagination of the objects of the world of form serve as moulds in which to hold, channels in which to canalise, the subtle forces that would otherwise prove too elusive to handle. These subjective images are the link between form and force, and they are very important in occult practice. One can safely say that the person who cannot use the visual imagination cannot do magic, and the better a person can visualise, the better magician will he be.

This art of visualisation is employed in meditation until expertness is arrived at, and then it is given a further definiteness and concentration by being combined with action on the physical plane. Thus is developed a ceremonial with mind power behind it - the mind-work that brings power into a ceremony, and the ceremony that gives concentration to mind-work. If we ask which is done first, we are but proposing a new version of the old question, "Which came first, the hen or the egg?" When the man with a trained mind works a ceremony, there is an immediate influx of power into the ceremony, and as he works the ceremony, there is an influx of power into himself and he works with enhanced power. It is the syphon principle, whereby water running out of a pipe draws water into the pipe. An even more illuminating analogy is found in the system of pulleys and blocks that can be used to magnify the energy exerted, but that, without the exertion of some energy, would be inert.

We have then, in magic, a device for controlling subtle invisible forces that are behind the world of form as it is known to us; these forces are controlled by freeing the corresponding level of consciousness from the bondage of the world of form, but at the same time retaining it under control, like a horse on a lunging rein. The mind is freed by training in meditation, and kept under control by means of ceremonial.

By means of the discipline of specially designed and graded meditations the mind is habituated to the exercise of a higher mode of consciousness than that which is developed in it by the experiences of the senses; and with the development of this higher mode of consciousness it becomes conscious of higher things. A whole new world opens to it - the world of the subtle forces behind appearances, which we know must be there, yet which we have as yet found no way of assessing save in the subtle reactions of the mind of the psychic.

If the development brought about by the occult training were limited to the development of psychism alone, the initiate would in no way differ from any other psychic; but in addition to learning to perceive these forces, he also aims at acquiring control over them. To this end he uses the different factors in his own nature as the man-power that is put behind the pulley and block, and he uses his ceremonial as the tackle and ring-bolt with which he lays hold of the particular type of cosmic force which corresponds to the factor in his own nature that he has applied to the work of magic.

It will thus be seen how the three factors enter into the operation - mind power, the astral forms, and the cosmic forces.

If these principles be applied to the consideration of that example of ceremonial magic with which everyone is familiar - the Eucharist, it will be seen that they are represented by the faith of the worshipper, the Real Presence, and the power of the Cosmic Christ. Be it noted also the stress laid by the Catholic upon the Real Presence, and the consequent potency of his Mass; and the denial by the Protestant of the miracle of Transubstantiation, and the relative inertness of his Holy Communion. From this we learn a very important lesson in the practical art of magic - we must believe in the equivalent of the Real Presence in any operation, or our magic will be inert, the Real Presence being that of the Angel of the Operation, the elemental spirit invoked, the Master of the Degree, or whatever may be the astral form that is built up by the magical mind as the channel of power that conveys the subtle to the dense. Have faith in the coming of a Real Presence, of whatever nature, and power comes into your rite. Disbelieve it as a mere ignorant superstition or rationalise it away, and your ceremony will be inert.

Believe in it superstitiously, and you will be haunted by bugaboos; but understand the power of the thought-form to bring through a cosmic force that ensouls and renders it real and potent, and you have the means of performing the miracle of Transubstantiation upon whatever symbol you elect to use. Make your thought-form after the appropriate manner, and the corresponding force will ensoul it and you have a Real Presence.

This constitutes the technique of magic, and is applied to whatever matter is in hand. The magical operations themselves are differentiated not by method, for the same method is adapted to all the different processes, but by the end to which they are directed, which may be the initiating of a candidate, the charging of a talisman, or the energising of the mind and the enlarging of the experience of the operator.

Chapter 10b

THE PURPOSE OF MAGIC
Gareth Knight

To understand the purpose of magic we need first to understand the world view of the magician. This differs from the assumptions that are generally current in the modern intellectual climate. However, the magical world view is one of considerable antiquity and respectability, serving human cosmic speculation well before the time of Aristotle, through medieval times and on into the Renaissance. Since the middle of the seventeenth century the magical view of the universe has gradually given place to a more materialist conception, encouraged by the benefits of technology that have accrued from a rigorous application of the scientific method. Yet scientific discoveries that may validly have changed our views about the way the physical world is put together, do not necessarily invalidate the old conceptions regarding the existence and the structure of the psychic and spiritual worlds.

To put things in their simplest terms, the magician reckons to live in a three tier universe. One that is divided into the spiritual, the psychic and the physical.

The physical world is that world of teeming phenomena of which we are conscious by means of the sensory organs of our physical body and sometimes with the assistance of scientific instruments. The atheistic materialist considers that this is all that exists.

The spiritual world is the bosom and being of the Creator, the One, the Only Begetter of all that is, and our own souls into the bargain. The religions of the world seek to bring the individual soul into a rightful relationship with God, who, by definition, comprises all we can conceive of a spiritual world. They do this by means of systems of belief that are expressed in various acts of worship and of codes of living, the details of which vary according to contemporary culture.

The psychic world is that which lies between the physical and the spiritual. The unbeliever will deny that any such world exists, save in an entirely subjective sense that can be investigated according to the laws of psychology. The more liberal of the religiously orthodox in the Judaeo/Christian/Islamic traditions may well go along with this materialistic view. The more conservative, however, may well admit that an objective psychic world exists but will regard it as forbidden territory, fraught with traps and dangers and demonic forces.

The magician believes that this psychic world exists but declines to regard it as forbidden territory, but rather as a large and unknown country that is there to be explored. As with any physical exploration there are various means by which this can be undertaken and various motives for doing so.

At one extreme is the attempt to explore the psychic worlds with the same experimental rigour as in the pursuit of physical science, and using physical apparatus. Such were the intentions of the Society for Psychical Research, founded in the nineteenth century, where an extensive archive has been built up but one which by its very nature remains very close to the limitations of physical science. For the psychic realm to be explored in any depth then psychic means have to be employed, which, for the rigorous physical scientist, are too subjective to be seriously considered.

One can sympathise with the scientists' reservations in light of the considerable amount of self deception and superstition that is all too often evident in psychic circles. And apart from this, accuracy of observation depends upon the accuracy of our faculties of psychic perception, and these are more subject to error than our physical faculties (not that these are by any means infallible, as is revealed by conflicting accounts of witnesses in courts of law).

Also, what we meet within the psychic realms will be largely conditioned by our own attitude as participators or observers. A fundamental law of the psychic realm also is that Like attracts Like. This means that when we approach the psychic world we are going to be met with a close reflection of our own expectations. If we assume that all we meet there is going to be of the devil, then certainly some mirror images of our own fear-ridden prejudices may be expected. Those, on the other hand, who approach these realms in a state of high mystical expectation may well find themselves apparently raised into colloquy with saints and with angels.

As to motivation, if we approach this realm looking for what we can profitably exploit in material terms, like empire builders of old, then we are likely to meet up with similar opportunist exploiters and scavengers upon the inner planes. These may perhaps themselves be looking for vicarious thrills through the overshadowing of some personality still in incarnation. This is the basis of the traditions of the earth-bound, or of the incubus and succubus - feeding upon sexual acts and fantasies. Other yobbish entities may get a charge from vicarious violence, which is at the root of mob law. This is a pooling of auras in a very magical way that does not call for sophisticated magical techniques, for it happens instinctively. Different types of music and theatrical performance attract a similar interaction between the planes. The performing arts, good and bad, are very magical acts, for magic is a universal phenomenon and in its broader sense far from being confined to a few esoteric specialists.

With this in mind, we may perhaps see why puritan enthusiasts in olden days tried instinctively to ban theatrical performances.

They can be an opening of the gates of the psychic world, and sometimes in none too salubrious a fashion. A High Church mass would have figured high in their detestation, for a religious service with ritual, apart from its spiritual element, can have a significant magical content.

The spiritual element of any religious service may be considered as a level set apart from any magical or psychic aspects. This is because there is a direct relationship between spiritual intention and physical activity resulting therefrom, which transcends any psychic or magical considerations. It is this that justifies the theological teaching that the administration of the sacraments are valid no matter what the moral standing or mental preoccupations of the priest.

This is a ruling open to cynical criticism, the more so because in magical and psychic affairs, the personal performance and integrity of those concerned is crucial to success. However, the magical or psychic element within any divine service fall into an intermediate level similar to the degree of upliftment that may be felt according to the way that the organ is played or how well the choir sings.

A religious service is therefore not aimed at working magic, although some forms of prayer may well come close to certain types of magic, at any rate in intent. Those, for instance, that seek specific physical intervention or intercession by particular saints into the peoples' lives. Conversely, it is very rare that a magical ceremony is intended to be simply an act of worship.

Personal enlightenment is one aim of ceremonial magic, but the overall purpose is not limited to psychological self help, even if with a spiritual dimension. The ethic of the Western Esoteric Tradition, which includes ritual magic among its other disciplines, is encapsulated in the aspiration: "I desire to know in order to serve."

Initiates, by means of their specialisation of being able to open the gates to the inner worlds, (of which there are many modes and levels, each with their particular type of intelligence) seek to cooperate with those they find there. This means they may be impressed to perform particular actions, or to design and perform particular rituals under inner plane advice and direction.

Examples of this in terms of directed visualisations are to be found in the war letters of Dion Fortune, selected extracts of which with a commentary by me have been published under the title of *The Magical Battle of Britain*. For a more recent example, however, and one that involves field work and ritual practice, we may turn to a continuation of the Chapel of Remembrance work already mentioned in these pages.

In the week prior to the eightieth anniversary of the Battle of the Somme it seemed important for me, together with the initiate who had been working on this material, to visit some of the battle sites and the related war graves. This was an intuitive impulsion that came almost completely out of the blue, aided by favourable circumstances developing, and we were indeed not previously aware that major anniversary celebrations were intended or that they were so close.

During the course of this visit we discovered the traditions surrounding the town of Albert which lies in the midst of this region. In medieval times, so legend has it, a shepherd discovered a buried golden statue of the Virgin holding the Christ child aloft before her. A basilica was built for it in the local town of Albert, which, in the course of time, became a centre for pilgrimage, even being called "the Lourdes of the North". Upon its spire was a large replica of the golden virgin and child.

In the course of the Great War the basilica was severely damaged but the golden madonna at the top remained in place, leaning over at a crazy angle, as if offering her child to the war torn town and battle fields below. It became quite an object of piety and indeed superstition at the time for troops on both sides. It was said that when it finally fell the war would end. It did finally fall in 1918 after the last German push when the tower was finally demolished by British artillery to prevent it being used as an observation post for the German army. Since then the whole church has been rebuilt and refurbished complete with golden virgin and child at its summit.

There came to us independently the realisation that this golden virgin was a very important magical image related to the continuing need for some channel of release and absolution to souls of victims of war who might still be entrapped in the horrors they had experienced. Accordingly, on our return to England we arranged to work a ritual along these lines, and an opportunity came do so within the following week, just prior to the official anniversary ceremonies.

We had no hard and fast idea of exactly what was required, except in most general terms. Accordingly, the set up we chose was very simple, with just two officers, one in the East and the other in the West. After a brief opening by my colleague in the East, I, as Western officer outlined the purpose of the working and explained the legend and later story of the golden virgin of Albert. The Eastern officer then conducted a guided visualisation very much along the lines of the description of the Chapels of Remembrance that we have earlier quoted. We agreed that this would be followed by an extemporary working by the Western officer, according to whatever seemed to be appropriate at the time by the inner plane forces set flowing.

As it happened, this turned out to be virtually a summons and exorcism of release for the entrapped souls of fallen soldiers. In our visits to military cemeteries, kept immaculate by the War Graves Commission, we had been struck by the atmosphere of peace and calm that prevailed. However, at certain other battlefield sites this was often far from the case, a different atmosphere prevailed. Waves and patches of fear and horror were still perceptible, sometimes general depression to an overbearing degree. One was indeed reminded of filmed sequences to be seen in the war museum at Peronne of the effect of shell shock upon some of those who survived, which were more moving and horrifying than the worst of physical injuries displayed. What, one might have asked, of those who were so shocked but died in action? Have they yet achieved release from their introverted horror? Some part of an answer to this may be provided in the spontaneous working that followed.

There came into my mind, very strongly, a formula that is sometimes used in jest at the end of re-enactments of ancient battles by military historical societies. Those who have fallen in simulated death on the field are bidden to get up and go by the phrase "Let the dead arise!"

Indeed I can recall the hair standing up on the back of my neck when this formula was used, on site, at the millennial celebrations of the Battle of Maldon. Little did the holiday crowd, or the evocatively voiced lady commentator realise, but rising they certainly were, Saxon and Viking. I had a very disturbed night, particularly conscious of the state of mind of the leader of the Saxon defence force, Byrhtnoth, who seemed overcome with remorse about the tactics he had adopted that day, allowing the Vikings to cross a causeway in order to fight a pitched battle, that ended in victory for the invaders.

So magic is where you find it and will operate, from inner levels, irrespective of the conscious realisations of many of those involved. I offer no explanations regarding the passage of inner plane time or after death conditions of ancient warriors, I simply state what I experienced with my inner faculties, and if any should think that this is all simply part of an over-heated and romantic imagination then they are quite entitled to that view. But that is but one hypothesis amongst many.

As it happened on that occasion, a religious service had been arranged for the following day to dedicate a memorial window of the battle in a local church. By one of those serendipities that often occur in this type of work, the service incorporated a visiting specialist choir, who sang an ancient Anglo Saxon form of the mass. To my perceptions, this acted as a powerful aid in putting many of those who had been evoked the previous day to rest or release. I imagine the congregation and visiting dignitaries thought the ceremony to be simply a quaint and recherché way of celebrating a civic event, but to the magical eye there was much more to it than that.

However, to return to the Somme related working, it came to me that I should stand at each of the quarters in turn and state this formula, elaborated into "Let the dead arise! Let the un-dead arise!" with the direction that they were now free to go. As I did so, to inner perception, the western wall of the lodge seemed to open in a blaze of glory to reveal the golden virgin of Albert holding up her golden child, and with this the words of an old recruiting song came to mind: "We don't want to lose you, but we think you ought to go!" In modern retrospect, the words and sentiments of this song seem quite revolting, inciting as they did, young men to go to their slaughter by an arch innuendo of sexuality. However, in the context of the intentions of the ritual, they took on another dimension in their meaning. Just as those who might have received white feathers from young ladies as an encouragement to prove their manhood and enlist might now receive the feathers of angels' wings at the hands of the Virgin of Albert. At this point the officer of the East began, spontaneously to sing the words of this song.

Whatever objective good may have been done in this working, it was certainly a powerful experience for me, and indeed also for others as extracts from some of the lodge reports below signify. They give some indication of the type and level of power that was running in the lodge at the time, together with the confirmation that the work was not simply related to the Battle of the Somme, but by extension to the fallen of all wars.

(i) *"the work...impromptu though it was, seemed to have struck the right chord. The feeling I had was of hundreds, perhaps thousands of 'stuck' souls saying to each other 'It's OK, we can go now'. And they were saying this not only in English, but in German and French, in Yankee and Confederate accents, in tones of Royalist and Roundhead;*

in Russian and Polish, Japanese and Chinese, Serbian and Croat, Irish and English, Chinese, Japanese, Vietnamese, and American..."

(ii) *"S..... sang beautifully and there followed an extremely vivid inner scene of `the dead and undead` rising from the mud, at first in utter disbelief, then forward with hesitation and then with a rush which came through to the physical as an actual movement of air."*

(iii) *"As the souls of the dead and the undead were summoned from the quarters and around the circle, there was a tremendous build up of power and the sense of the gathering of entities, and as the working continued, and the western officer called up the souls, and the eastern officer began to sing, the Great Western Gates drew wide open and there was the sound of marching and they went through in their thousands. The singing from the East really brought them forward as the officer became a kind of spiritual 'forces sweetheart' linking in with the figure of the Golden Virgin and calling them to the New Western Front. (Eat your heart out Vera Lynn!)"*

(iv) *"The working itself invoked a great feeling of peace in the lodge, that then turned 'ballistic' as the soldiers were called forth. (Sitting in the north I felt as if someone suddenly connected me to a live wire). I was also aware of the elemental kingdoms and the effect this war had on them, as well as other events concerning the misuse and abuse of power. I wondered if they should be included in some way during this working, but as I considered this one of the Masters appeared and informed me that they now could deal with this by utilising the pattern we had set up."*

(v) *"The Somme working was incredibly moving and seemed to operate at a deep level for me. I found I was very tearful afterwards and for the last week have had flashes and parts of dreams relating to the Somme/WW1. I found myself switching on relevant TV programmes last week and want to do some related reading."*

(vi) *"The Somme working was mind blowing. A kind of neopolitan ice-cream effect - four different inner plane pictures superimposed upon each other - the outer temple, the inner abbey, the war cemeteries as I had seen them as a teenager, and a happy laughing joking throng of*

'Tommies' walking away to freedom. When the Western door of the abbey opened, I literally got cold shivers up my spine."

(vii) *"Undoubtedly it was very powerful and was certainly the main purpose of our weekend's work and of opening the gateway to the West. I sat in the lodge room prior to going to bed and it was positively buzzing with energy."*

(viii) *"I was aware of a great deal of action in the matter of battlefield resurrection. And the message seemed to be getting passed on by the troops involved, either from comrade to comrade, or sergeant majors and other NCO's arousing their fallen men as if for reveille, even a whole (or part of what remained of) a whole cavalry troop rose from the mud and galloped off. And this kept on going on, and I would think did so all night."*

(ix) *"I have to admit that I went into this working with very little idea of what it was all about - no rehearsal and very little prior discussion - and not expecting it to be very powerful. But the spontaneity and lack of formality and organisation seemed to substantially enhance the power that came through. It was when I was going round lighting the quarter candles, and felt a great surge of force following the light round the Lodge, that I realised we were in for a real humdinger. There also seemed to be a line of force going across the Lodge from East to West, like a great cosmic magnet. One experience I had during this working which I've never had before was the sudden disappearance of my visual imagination. I lost all concept of inner vision and my consciousness seemed to comprise only solid blocks of pure feeling. I mean, I've reached altered states of consciousness before in meditations and rituals but this was something else again. The only visual image I had - and an astonishingly strong one at that - was of the Western doors of the church flying open (whether it was the Basilique at Albert or some other I couldn't say) and all the dead soldiers trekking out with their rifles and packs towards a magnificent red-gold sunset over a green field, with the Golden Virgin towering massively into the sky and welcoming them with open arms. And after that I couldn't see anything; I just had this sensation of pure consciousness without verbal or visual thought. After the working I had to go and sit in the* *garden for twenty minutes to recover from it; I felt really strange. I shall never forget the experience of doing this working as long as I live."*

Another report is worth particular attention as it records relevant impressions some hours **before** the rite was worked, during the general opening ceremony to the weekend's work.

(x) *"I felt the opening ritual was being used (either by my subconscious or by inner plane entities) to provide information on what was on the menu for the rest of the day. I knew I was picking up material that was not strictly relevant to the opening itself.*

"In the East, the Unknown Soldier of 1st and 2nd World Wars, in fatigues. He represents a body of men who died for their idealism and have since become inner plane initiates working from the other side. They need something from us. It would appear to be a ritualised form of acknowledgement of their existence in this capacity and to make a link between earthly initiates and them. In the West, Sophia as a blazing light, the light of inner plane wisdom coming to meet, or rising up in sympathetic polarity with the Unknown Soldier.

"These two figures could just have been precognitive, purely psychic images, rather than objective inner plane presences utilising images, (there is a difference!). However, the fact that the Unknown Soldier radiated more material than actually arose in the subsequent spontaneous working, makes me incline toward the objective inner plane presence. Certainly he required me to relate to him during the later working as a potently real spirit. I had a strong sense of overshadowing by the Virgin in order to mediate love in the face of desperation.

"So when the doors were opened in the west I expected the Virgin/ Sophia to appear and felt all was going to plan. The soldier seemed more whole, more healed by the end. There was a sense of the achieved Grail about him, and at this point, as before, the reality of a band of inner plane adepti specifically drawn from the ranks of those who died in WW1 (& 2) reasserted itself.

"This lot wish to be known. They wish us to know such a brotherhood exists, and that they exist to work for peace in a dynamic, strong, incisive way as an inner plane force who can be

contacted and used to provide inspiration, initiative and push for peace and the environment. There was the suggestion that they are `behind` the green warriors of Greenpeace etc. The name `The Light of the Somme` came to mind. I don't know how reliable all this is, but I pass it on for people to make what they will of it.

"Approaching all this intellectually, I would have thought that there had been more than enough religious intercession and prayer for the soldiers of the world wars, but I fear that war being such an endless activity and generating so many countless casualties, there is a virtually ceaseless line of confused and tormented souls waiting to come through for healing etc., should an appropriate gate be opened. I am not sure to what extent we are really dealing with any specific group of people. It may be the Somme is itself being used as a useful magical image."

All of the above is a sample of one particular magical ritual. One could have chosen from dozens of others but this one, for various reasons, seems particularly appropriate to quote. And on the favourite dictum of Dion Fortune that an ounce of practice is worth a pound of theory, this little bit of practical magic recently performed may perhaps serve to show to some extent at least one of the purposes of magic in one particular line of the tradition.

APPENDIX A

TALISMANIC MAGIC
Dion Fortune

Talismanic magic is an intrinsic part of the ceremonial art in general, and cannot be considered apart therefrom; but being a special application of that art, it is entitled to special consideration.

If a sacrament is the outward and visible sign of an inward and spiritual grace, a talisman may be considered as the material object in which the inward and spiritual grace is stored. A talisman is, in fact, nothing more or less than a spiritual storage battery. The manner in which a talisman works is difficult to define, but the fact that it works is a matter of experience. After we have considered the technique of the making of talismans we shall be in a better position to examine the principles involved and deduce an explanation of the nature and manner of operating talismanic magic.

If an occultist wants to draw to himself power of a particular type, or to stimulate a particular factor in his nature, he will start by analysing that factor into its primary principles and assign it to its particular station upon the Tree of Life. For instance, all operations of a combative, or defensive nature would be assigned to Geburah, the Sphere of Mars; all those of an artistic or emotional nature to Netzach, the Sphere of Venus.

Having thus classified his problem, he would then study the symbolism of that Sephirah according to the traditional significance assigned to it.

Having got clearly in his mind a concept of the nature of the force in question, he will next consider its opposite aspect that maintains it in equilibrium; for instance, the opposite aspect of Netzach upon the Tree is Hod, the Sphere of Mercury, the intellectual as opposed to the artistic; the opposite aspect of Geburah is Chesed, the Sphere of Jupiter, the benign law-giver, organiser and preserver. He will then understand how the force he desires must be balanced and held in equilibrium. Finally, he will consider its Qlippotic manifestation, that is to say, its nature when unbalanced and degenerated. He will then have a clear understanding of the whole problem and be able to see it in perspective against the background of the cosmos as a whole, and he will also know the pathologies he has to guard against, and in what direction the force is liable to go if it becomes unbalanced. For instance, the Qlippah corresponding to Geburah is the Sphere of Burners, for unbalanced Geburic force leads to cruelty and destruction. It is very necessary to make this careful analysis of the problem before proceeding to the construction of a talisman, otherwise one may make bad worse by intensifying the trouble. The quarrelsome man, for instance, who has already got too much Geburah in his composition, might try to invoke more Geburah in order to get himself out of the hot water that his quarrelsomeness has got him into. Whereas what he needs is a talisman for Chesed, Mercy, the opposite quality to Geburah. If he draws in more Geburah when he has already got too much Geburah, the result is Qlippotic.

Having arrived at a clear understanding of what he intends to do, and knowing that he will have to shoulder the responsibility of any mistakes he may make should he have failed to diagnose his problem correctly, the operator then proceeds to design his talisman. Certain geometrical forms, colours, letters, numbers and many other things are associated with every type of cosmic force; these are classified into thirty-two types, corresponding to the ten Holy Sephiroth upon the Tree of Life, representing ten types of primary force, and the twenty-two Paths that connect them; these are classed as secondary or derivative forces, arising from the equilibrium of the pairs of Sephiroth they connect; they did not emanate directly from the Source of All Force, but were generated in the course of the development of the different Sephiroth; the Sephirotic forces are spiritual in type, but the influences of the Twenty-two Paths must be termed astral, for want of a better expression. In any talisman, therefore, the Sephirotic aspect will be the spiritual influence, and the specific mundane application will be sought in the symbolism of the appropriate Path; if the diagnosis has been correctly made, it should be one of the Paths connected with the selected Sephiroth. The symbolism will then be inter-related.

A talisman is best made of either parchment, which is the dressed skin of an animal, or sheet metal, for experience shows that these hold the magnetism better than ordinary paper. It is interesting to note that the substances that have been traditionally used from time immemorial are those which modern science knows to be good conductors of electricity. The substances, such as silk or wood, in which tradition instructs us to encase our talismans in order to conserve their energy, are the same that modern science has proven to be effectual as non-conductors. The old adepts said: "Do not use ordinary paper for a talisman, as it will not hold the force." The modern mechanic knows that there is nothing better than a piece of paper as an emergency insulator if he has to deal with a live wire.

There is an elaborate system of attribution of the metals to the different planets - gold to the sun, silver to the moon, iron to Mars - and theoretically, talismans for a particular force should be made from the appropriate metal. In actual practice, however, this is not feasible; the solid gold talisman of the sun is beyond the means of all save millionaires; the lead talisman of Saturn is too weighty to practical use; the iron talisman of Mars is liable to rust. The simplest and most practical method is to use a copper base enamelled with the symbolic colours.

And this brings us to the question of the nature of the efficacy of talismans. Why should a talisman be made of lead, or tin, or gold, according to the force it is designed to carry? In what way does it influence the force, or the force influence it?

In the present state of the exact science, our knowledge of the occult arts is largely empirical. That some sort of subtle electrical factor enters into the matter there is good reason to believe, for tradition instructed its students to deal with magical forces after the manner of an electrical installation thousands of years before anything was known of electricity. There are many weird and wonderful recipes in folklore and witchcraft that have no value save the psychological one of prolonging attention and generating emotion by the ready means of fear and horror, but when we find traditional practices in accordance with an electrical analogy, we are justified in assuming that they are based upon practical experience in handling a force of an electrical nature. It is extremely probable that recently developed instruments for magnifying and measuring electrical charges of very low potency would yield some very interesting results if applied to magic.

We may be justified in speculating that subtle electrical changes do take place when an amulet or talisman is charged; and that these are due to the personal magnetism of the person consecrating it. That personal magnetism is heightened by ceremonial work is a fact well known by experience to those who practise the occult arts.

We may therefore conclude that the use of an electrically active material out of which to make a talisman has a basis in experience. But what shall we say of the colours, symbols and names that go to make up the talisman itself? These can have no electrical effect one way or the other. In my opinion, their importance is psychological, but in a more extended sense than that term is generally understood.

Let us consider an analogy. In an electrical power station, the switch-box, in addition to the word: DANGER! may have a skull and cross-bones painted on it in bright scarlet, thus causing even the most scatter-brained to pause and think. Now why is the skull and cross-bones a more potent symbol than the word DANGER and why is scarlet paint more effective than black? Because skulls and skeletons are associated in our minds with death, and red with blood.

So it is with the magical symbols. Even the uninitiated associates these odd looking scribbles with power. To the initiated, "conditioned" to symbolism, they convey a sense of a particular kind of power. A talisman is only effective when the person who makes it has performed meditations upon each of the symbols inscribed upon it, so that they are full of significance for him. In making these meditations, he builds up a thought-form in the astral light corresponding to each force thus dealt with. When he inscribes a symbol on the talisman, this thought-form he has made is associated with it; thus is the astral light being a link with the cosmic force represented. If he has not performed such work as this, and the symbols have no real significance for him, the resulting talisman will have no more than a superstitious value as giving rise to auto-suggestion.

The real value of a talisman lies in the work that is put into it; therefore second-hand talismans made by someone else are only of use to the superstitious, like the quack medicines bought at fairs. But there is no question about it that the mental work that goes to the making of a talisman has a very real effect upon the personality, definitely energising it in the chosen direction, and that the power thus generated goes far beyond the influence of a purely subjective auto-suggestion.

Let this be noted, however - it is not the talisman that is doing the work, but the energy that has been put into the talisman. Miracles do not happen, if, by a miracle we understand an arbitrary interference with the natural sequence of cause and effect; magic, in my experience, always works through natural channels, its efficacy lying in the increase of energy that it causes to flow in those channels. If you make a talisman for wealth, you will not find a shower of golden sovereigns falling around it, but you may, and very probably will find that opportunities for increasing your earning power will come your way, and provided your temperament is sufficiently energised to enable you to take advantage of them, you will, by means of the normal channels, achieve prosperity - the normal channels being sound judgement, adequate skill, and hard work over a prolonged period. If you think to acquire anything in heaven, earth, or the Qlippotic waters under the earth by other channels than these, talismanic magic will prove of no more use than appeals to rich relations. Talismanic magic will give you energy, as can be readily understood in the light of the psychology of auto-suggestion; it will give you also opportunity, as can only be understood in the light of occult hypotheses, but it cannot enable you to avail yourself of that opportunity by any means save your own capacities.

A talisman is like any apparatus for physical culture - the developer does not develop your muscles, it is your use of it that develops them.

APPENDIX A

TALISMANIC MAGIC
Gareth Knight

In a sense all ritual magic is talismanic magic, and this could be extended to saying that all life properly and spiritually lived is also talismanic magic. That is to say, something that has spiritual power and validity is expressed upon the earth in material terms, whether in objects, words or actions.

The simplest form of talisman, that of the lucky charm, whilst of no great intrinsic spiritual significance or inner power, can nonetheless have its worth as an aid to self confidence. I recall that in childhood an enamel Cornish Pisky bought whilst on holiday was a great comfort for some period of time, including the early days of war, aided by the fact that it seemed to turn up again in unlikely circumstances if lost. And indeed the quasi-social element in children's dolls and toys will have a certain magical element within them. By virtue of their belief and vivid imagination children make natural magicians. .

There is also a talismanic element in ritual objects, even if they have not been consciously worked upon in a magical fashion. Thus, as an example in the Somme ritual already cited, a few relevant objects placed upon the altar certainly seemed to aid the conscious atunement of the group. Chosen by the officiating officer because they 'felt right', they included a red and a white rose, a large clod of dried mud from the Somme, her grandfather's war medal, the cloth poppies used in a previous ritual, and regimental badges of the two regiments in which Wilred Owen served - the Artists Rifles and the Manchester Regiment - bought from the war museum in Albert. The latter, an officer's cap badge, still had mud on it and had clearly been picked up from the battlefield, which does not bode well for the fate of its original owner.

Thus a talismanic significance may attach to objects associated with a particular location, although this should not be taken as an incitement to chip pieces off sacred sites. A souvenir bought at the associate tourist shop may prove just as effective and untainted by associations of personal vandalism.

A similar mechanism attaches to the religious practice of revering the relics of saints. It was held for a very long time, and still is in some religious quarters, that an altar is invalid unless it contains some holy relics. There may well be a strong subjective element in all of this, for by no means all saintly relics are genuine, and there have probably been enough fragments of the True Cross to account for the felling of a sizeable forest. Yet belief in the reality and power of relics has inspired some remarkable acts of bravery. For instance, at the siege of Antioch, when in their last extremity the crusaders convinced themselves that the original Holy Lance had been found. Upon the strength of this they marched out of the city, whereupon the besieging Turks fled in amazement, thus probably changing the course of history.

However, talismanic magic is also found in less remarkable circumstances. The Roman baths at Bath for instance provide a rich treasure trove of personal curses written on lead and dumped into the waters in supplication to the local gods, an act of splenetic piety probably widespread in those times.

A converse belief in talismanic power in medieval times was that if a fragment of a consecrated host could be secreted away from the mass, it would be a powerful ingredient in certain spells. It is thus perhaps small wonder that the church took a jaundiced view of the practice of witchcraft and magic, and throws a very pragmatic light on the assumptions of medieval piety.

It is also in the annals of the darker side of sorcery that nail or hair trimmings, or articles of clothing of an intended victim will act as a magical or talismanic link. This has a more positive side when used by modern day dowsers, when some hair from a lost dog may help in trying to trace the fate of the animal. Or on the occult principle that like attracts like, that a specimen of a substance being divined for be placed within a hollow pendulum bob.

However, in traditional magical manuals, talismans are usually associated with strange symbols written on parchment or inscribed upon metal plates. This formed part of the elementary curriculum of the Hermetic Order of the Golden Dawn, and in his remarks on the Order whose teachings he did so much to publicise, Israel Regardie considered it to be the easiest form of magic to work and one of the best introductory exercises in the art.

The symbols used are usually personally contrived ones. Conformed by the use of magic squares or other symbolic devices, names or short invocations can be encapsulated into symbolic diagrams. Sometimes these may be copied out of ill understood and defectively copied ancient works, and though this may provide a certain frisson to the latter day copyist, is likely to be less effective than working from first principles, using one's own intelligence. Taking in someone else's dirty washing is not a good idea in magical practice anyway, and the ingenuity and effort involved in designing one's own hieroglyphs as well as neatly inscribing them in a small compass on an expensive and intractable material, will certainly have some kind of magical effect.

There is indeed a talismanic effect in simply writing something down, and whilst this does not make an ordinary shopping list into a magical object, to go to the trouble of formulating a resolution or aspiration in words and then making a neat and specific note of it, probably has more effect than is generally realised. The business world has gone part way to realising this in the common injunction to executives to work out and specify their objectives. The business diary, or even wall planner, may seem a somewhat prosaic object but may not be entirely without a certain talismanic significance.

A permanently set up temple is certainly a powerful talisman within its own right and the same may be said of any particular ritual. Although it is of finite duration in time, effectively performed, it may well leave a pattern upon the higher ethers which can be utilised by other magical workers, including inner plane ones. In fact this is probably the main purpose of any major work of ceremonial white magic.

We have already drawn attention to the talismanic element in certain religious artefacts, and this is taken to its ultimate expression in an exemplary holy life. This is not simply a matter of concern to enclosed religious communities, but applies to the lives, not only of saints, but of "great" men and women in all walks of life. There was a time when history was considered to be the study of great human beings as examplars or paradigms.

To the Christian of course, none more so than the life of Christ. In this respect the life of Jesus seen as a sacramental act, redeeming the fallen creation, is a supreme example of talismanic magic - even if most theologians would feel uneasy at the term. And by the same terms a very talismanic mystical text is Thomas a Kempis' *The Imitation of Christ*.

In a less religious but very important sense the principle was also formulated by the great Victorian man of letters, Thomas Carlyle. In *Heroes and Hero Worship* he gave examples of exemplary lives. His list included Mahomet (the hero as prophet), Dante and Shakespeare (the hero as poet), Luther and Knox (the hero as priest), Johnson, Rousseau and Burns (the hero as man of letters), Cromwell and Napoleon (the hero as king). A somewhat arbitrary selection perhaps, andnot a shopping list of individuals to whom all of us can aspire, but in the sense of the expression of the spiritual potential of the human species over a wide range of human activity, we could certainly call the life of the hero one of talismanic significance.

This is a dynamic that occurs in certain types of ceremonial magic when particular human qualities or national aspirations may be encapsulated in archetypal historical figures. The Elizabethan age is particularly rich in this kind of dynamic of which perhaps the most powerful in my experience has been that of Sir Francis Drake. Significant not only for his importance as a national naval hero but, in being the first ship's captain to circumnavigate the globe, might be called the first "planetary man". His physical actions signalled and confirmed a new epoch in human affairs.

As is typical in the cult of the hero his life has taken on mythopoeic accretions. Apart from the legend of Drake's drum which will bring about his return if struck when England is in danger, there is the legend of his soul overshadowing Nelson, and of his laying on a water supply for Plymouth by galloping his horse about Dartmoor to cause springs to rise, and of a cannon ball falling from heaven to prevent his fiancée marrying another while he was on his world voyage.

At the less spectacular level at which most of us conduct our affairs, we can live the talismanic life as good husbands, wives, fathers, mothers, friends, neighbours, employers, employees. This may sound rather more demanding or even boring than camping about in magical robes and writing symbols on fragments of parchment or discs of metal. Nonetheless it has its part in the magical life.

In reply to a question about what magical work we could undertake to try to make the world a safer and better place one of the masters recently replied:

The answer lies in right living. Set your own house in order and you will be setting up conditions for the rest to follow. It is rather as in a saturated solution of a potentially crystalline salt. If one molecule, or *small set of molecules, forms a crystalline structure, the rest will follow - and suddenly the amorphous liquid becomes a mass of scintillating crystals. Strive to be like that crystalline molecule. Of course, I cannot promise that all society will suddenly change, for human society is far from being in, or even near, the state of a `saturated` solution.*

But control what you have in your own Ring-Pass-Not in your own small cosmos, and because you will be expressing a fundamental cosmic pattern, or image of God or good, then it will have considerably more effect than you might realise.

Again, this is asking a lot. None of us are perfect - and to assume that we may be is to come close to the fall of Lucifer. But by doing the best we may, in all love and humility, and expressing ourselves as creatively as we can and should, we are contributing to the work of the light.

Rituals and ceremonies, or other acts or visualisations we ask you to do, have also an important place. But they are one facet in the whole of the crystal that you can and should express in your incarnate life in the world. In other words, be a good citizen, of inner and outer worlds, and as you are faithful in small things so will you achieve in great.

None of us of course is perfect, which gives the lie to the assumption that the magician is someone who lifts himself up by his own bootstraps to infinite power and virtue. The life of man in the sphere of Earth is one that is beset with problems, some of them insuperable. But that is no barrier to service. As this same master once said in an address given through Dion Fortune: "Learn to fail well!" In other words, pick yourself up, dust yourself down, and start all over again - without recrimination, despair or self pity. That is real talismanic magic.

In the more restricted sense of the term however, talismanic objects may also be an adjunct to magical rituals. One example of this in connection with the Chapels of Remembrance work came in the November following, the month particularly of remembrance, which in France sees two public holidays close together. The first Toussaint, or All Saints, when it is the custom for families to remember their dead, often travelling many miles to visit family graves with floral tributes, the second Armistice Day on the 11th of the month marked by ceremonies at war memorials and not least at the tomb of the Unknown Warrior at the Place d'Étoile in Paris.

By coincidence I happened to be in Paris upon this day and so went along to pay my respects, and there bought a "bleuet de France" from a flag seller, not having realised before that this was as important a commemorative flower for the French as the poppy is for us. Was it coincidental I ask myself that we had a stunning show of cornflowers (*bleuets*) in our garden this year, to go with the rose and geraniums from Picardy?

It also happened to be the full moon immediately prior to these dates that my colleague in this work found herself in Northern Ireland. When out on the Somme in June we visited the Ulster Tower, a memorial tower and chapel to the 36th (Ulster) Division, who went over the top on the first day of the Battle of the Somme and with spectacular gallantry captured five lines of German trenches within an hour. Unfortunately, owing to some confusion in the high command, the troops behind them failed to back them up, and they also found themselves being shelled by British artillery. Needless to say by the end of the day the Germans had come back and massacred them. The Ulster Tower is built on the site of the trenches where the Ulster Division came to grief and has become something of a site of pilgrimage for Irish people.

Sr. I.N.C. found the place particularly moving, and on a strong impulse waded into the remains of the old trenches and picked a handful of poppy seedheads which she brought back to England. Not really knowing what to do with them she collected the seeds in an old film canister and forget about them. However, on this particular weekend she unexpectedly found herself trekking off to Ulster and it became fairly clear that she was meant to take the poppy seeds over there and plant them. So, with a bit of grubbing around on a grass verge near Lough Neagh, she managed to fulfil what seemed to be an important esoteric act, linking up the Somme battlefield where the men of Ulster went down with Ulster itself by means of a living thing which, in itself a symbol of remembrance, has regenerated itself for eighty years on the battlefield and will hopefully continue to do so in Ireland.

APPENDIX B

ASTRAL FORMS
Dion Fortune

Among other things for which I have been chastised in various journals and groups is an account of my vision of a salamander that once appeared in the *Inner Light Magazine*.

If I had said that a salamander was present in the fire, I think there might be something, though not much, to be said against me; but as I only said I saw a salamander, the matter is on an entirely different footing. If I had said I had seen pink snakes or red rats, creatures whose existence is equally well authenticated, my statement would have been understood in the spirit in which it was made - that is to say, I perceived a phenomenon whose cause was remote and not immediate, and the point of real interest is: How did I perceive it? What was the stimulus that gave rise to the images in my mind?

Those who have had experience of psychic vision know that there are two types of images that appear before the mind's eye - the normal pictures in the imagination, and a certain other type of image which, though of just such a nature as the imagination pictures, have an altogether different type of validity.

The nature of that validity is very difficult to define as the flavour of a choice wine or tea or the merit of a gem; nevertheless, experienced persons have no difficulty in assessing it in trades where an error of judgement makes a difference of hundreds of pounds. There are certain objective standards in checking up the astral images, just as there are objective tests for weight and specific gravity, but for the most part it is a question of judgement, and the reliability of the trained senses - eye, palate, or psychism as the case may be. Experts will arrive at a pretty close consensus of opinion, save when commissioned for *ex parte* purposes; it is among the inexpert that a variegated assortment of opinion prevails.

Let me give an example from personal, practical experience. I am a Western-trained occultist, accustomed to work with the Qabalah and unfamiliar with Eastern systems. A belated interest having been aroused in the subject of yoga, I began to experiment. I knew there were seven chakras, but had only a hazy notion as to their location. I knew from the analogy of the Qabalistic Tree of Life that colours must be associated with them, but did not know what they were. It is interesting to note that I picked up the location of the chakras and their colours correctly, and as some of them have two, and even three colours, this could hardly be ascribed to guesswork. When I came to read the standard book on the subject, Arthur Avalon's *Serpent Power*, which I had not read prior to my experiments, I was amazed to find how many of the tricks of practical yoga I had picked up, working by myself and without guidance - a practice I should deplore in my students.

I have spent twenty years working at occultism, and nineteen of them have passed in asking myself whether the astral images seen by psychic vision are subjective or objective. I knew that one got results by using them, but whether one was getting anything more than the fruits of effective auto-suggestion, I did not know. I am by nature sceptical of the supernatural, and a training in psychoanalysis is not a thing to make one think nobly of the soul; my natural bias was to assess the astral images as beginning and ending subjectively, but the conviction has gradually been forced upon me that there is something more to them than that.

Much put off by Bishop Leadbeater's system of pipe-lines for relaying spiritual power, I swung to the other extreme, and interpreted everything in terms of abstract consciousness. In this I was encouraged by my Qabalistic studies, for the Qabalah expressly teaches that its very concrete system of imagery is purely symbolic, and the arrangement of the wig and whiskers of the Ancient of Days is not to be taken *au pied de la lettre*. I was further interested to see in studying Eastern systems in the original sources and not the Theosophical re-hashes of them, that it is states of consciousness and organisations of force that are being described, and not astral flora, fauna, and geography. This is brought out unequivocally on page 19 of Arthur Avalon's Introduction to *The Serpent Power*.

In view of the fact that both Eastern and Western systems of occultism, developing independently, use in their inner, secret side fundamentally the same methods, so that an initiate of one, in spite of prejudice, finds himself at home in the other, it appears to me that we are dealing with something more than arbitrary auto-suggestive symbols, with no more intrinsic value than Coué's little bit of knotted twine.

That the astral forms did not occupy positions in space as described by Bishop Leadbeater, I felt pretty certain; but that one got results by *visualising* them as occupying positions in space, I also knew. In brief, I learnt by experience that if one refined the superstition out of one's occultism, once ceased to get results.

Here I received, as I have often received, enlightenment from that very occult saint, Ignatius of Loyola, when he advised his Jesuits to work as if everything depended on work, and pray as if everything depended on prayer. In other words, if one wanted to get results in either magic or psychism, one had to operate *as if* the astral forms were three-dimensional, occupied position in space, and obeyed the laws of chemistry, physics and mechanics. At the same time, however, one had to bear in mind the metaphysical and psychological interpretation of all the phenomena in order to correlate it with normal experience and keep one's hold on reality. It was, in fact, between the Devil and the deep sea of being obsessed by one's own credulity or nullified by one's own scepticism. Of the two, it is better, I think, and certainly more efficacious, to err on the side of credulity; for if sufficiently credulous, one can always get a fellow charlatan to do an exorcism if the astral images get out of hand; whereas there is nothing I know of that can start up the works of scepticism.

So far as I can judge, what we perceive as the astral images are the reactions the mind makes to certain non-physical stimuli. It perceives them as three-dimensional and occupying space because that is the way it is accustomed to work and it does not know any other. It can be trained to dispense with the images and think in terms of pure idea, but this is a laborious task, whether undertaken by Yogi, Sufi, or Saint, and I am more and more inclined to doubt its value. In any case, it takes one right out of contact with this world; and though the experience may be very blissful to those that like that sort of thing, I doubt whether it is very beneficial to mind, body or estate.

It is, in my opinion, a very sound and useful test to ask oneself what would happen if everyone pursued a given course of action, and if the answer is that it would be disastrous or impractical, then the conclusion may be drawn that it is not right in principle for anyone to pursue it. If we were all just, if we were all kind, if we were all honest, the world would be a much better place; but if we were all Yogis sitting in perpetual meditation, it would be a singularly insanitary one, for who would empty the saints' slops?

By availing ourselves of the imagination's faculty for responding to non-physical stimuli, we retain the focusing, delimiting powers of the mind, which are its chief asset; discard them, and you might as well not have a mind, as we may observe in the case of a good many mystics. For all practical purposes it is immaterial to distinguish between the objectively motivated image, which is a true astral form, and the subjectively motived image, which is a picture in the imagination, just as it is immaterial in psychoanalysis whether a patient presents a genuine dream for psychoanalysis or a made-up one, for both are products of the psyche.

This may sound paradoxical, but it contains a very important practical point. After all, when you image a thing in your imagination, it exists on the astral, and is, therefore, an astral image, the astral plane being but another name for the collective subconscious, and the collective subconscious but another name for the astral plane. By definition, the collective subconscious is obviously something more than your or my individual subconscious, and therefore it has an objective as well as a subjective aspect for each of us. Our subconsciousness forming part of the collective subconscious, it follows, if we agree to identify the astral plane with the collective subconscious, that the astral plane has a subjective factor for each of us, and we are in fact hard put to it to say where our private subconsciousness ends and the public one begins.

Viewed in this way, we can see how the astral images can be at one and the same time both subjective and objective, and that the magician objectifies the subjective by projecting mental force, and the seer subjectifies the objective by letting the astral images rise by reflection in his imagination. The adept owes his powers to the fact that he has extended his consciousness into the subjective subconscious, and his grade depends upon the degree to which he is able to extend it.

By use of the astral images it is possible to get into touch with the invisible reality behind appearances without disorganising the concrete mind or losing touch with the objective world; and surely, as long as we have to share this objective world with relatives, neighbours, and fellow citizens, this is a thing we should aim at doing?

APPENDIX B

ASTRAL FORMS
Gareth Knight

The stock in trade of the practising occultist, and in particular the ritual magician, are images vividly held within the imagination. There is indeed a lot more to the spectrum of human consciousness, from the formless bliss of the mystic to the sheer physical *joie de vivre* of the dancer or athlete; from hard abstract mental thought of the scientist or mathematician to the emotional charge of performing or listening to music.

Yet a key to controlling a whole range of consciousness is by way of the evocation and manipulation of images. In this Dion Fortune's definition of magic as "the art of causing changes in consciousness in accordance with will" is directly relevant.

The modus operandi, the tuning dial of consciousness, is upon the level of what some will regard as subjective fantasy, and others as astral forms. But whatever terms we choose to use, from the magician's point of view the controlling element is the will. That is, we should control the images - not let the images control us.

Of course most of us do act as passive participators in a fantasy world for much of the time. It is what keeps the advertising industry in business, manipulating images that will appeal to us and stimulating our fantasy world. There is nothing inherently wrong with fantasy as long as it does not become a glamorous compulsion, seducing or dominating our will and our actions. Or in extreme cases feeding neurosis or psychosis. The mass murderer or sexual criminal are victims of their own compulsive fantasies before they start to seek victims in the outer world.

The magician is not unique in trying to work positively and creatively with fantasy. It is done by every creative artist, by every inventor, by every visionary business entrepreneur or politician. Perhaps closest to the way the magician uses this faculty is the writer of fiction or drama.

In trying to account for their creative process writers sometimes say that their characters "just seemed to take over", or "to take on a life of their own". There remain different attitudes by different writers to this kind of thing happening. Most seem to welcome it when it happens, although there is a strong body of opinion that considers it a mistake to let the characters have too much leeway. Some writers indeed warn against what they call this "quasi mystical" approach to the contents of the creative imagination.

A good middle ground would appear to be that once a good firm plot or framework for a novel has been shaped then it can be no bad thing for some of the characters to "come alive" and begin to act spontaneously within these prescribed but not too inflexible limits. This again, would be no bad formula for constructing a magical ritual.

The key issue in all of this is the status we are willing to grant these images within the imagination. They may appear to be inside our own heads but are capable of acting with considerable power.

To the creative writer they are the means for producing anything from a work of art to a saleable product. The writer is in control, and the end result is what goes down upon paper and survives the editing process. Although the success of the work may depend on how powerfully these images are rejuvenated in the minds of others. One thinks of famous characters in fiction that have become almost household names, from James

Bond to Mr Pickwick. This influence can be even greater in the medium of film and particularly upon the suggestible young. Here we start to move once more into the realms of advertising, promotion, public relations, spin doctoring, political propaganda and the various means of manipulating public opinion.

In all of this, the general assumption is that despite the way such images can cause people to act objectively in certain ways, the images themselves are at root subjective, and their action the field of the psychologist.

However, those who have experience of the occult world have a different set of assumptions. They believe there to be another level of objective reality beyond the realm of the images, if not in the images themselves.

Most of those involved insist that the results they achieve carry their own subjective proof, all be it not objectively demonstrable in scientifically controlled conditions. This is fair enough so far as it goes but the problem remains that they will interpret their experience in terms of beliefs already held.

Thus the spiritualists will interpret all that they experience in terms of personal communications with the recently departed. Early Theosophical Society researchers have tended to project the images into the physical environment, seeing great astral lights and forms emanating from churches or surrounding individuals in particular emotional states. (As in *Thought Forms* by Besant & Leadbeater). The magical ritualist will have another perspective on all this, through experiences whilst "on contact" within a particular ceremony. Thus, on occasion, officers working with Elizabethan historical images have felt themselves suddenly to be clothed in costume of the period interpreting this experience as best they may - as an overshadowing by an historical personality, or by a collective thought form, or some kind of archetype.

All the above witnessess are likely to refer to the images as Astral Forms, which is a useful enough term but, like so many in this realm, not always well defined. It assumes the existence of a mode of reality known as the Astral Plane. Some psychologists, notably Jungians, have their own catalogue of useful terms for this kind of thing, such as various Archetypes of the Unconscious for many of the forms, and Collective Unconscious for the realm from which they may emanate. These may or may not be terms synonymous with those used by occultists of various schools. Much depends upon the unstated assumptions of the individuals involved.

This does not mean to say, however, that all these people are deluded. It simply means that we do not have sufficiently accurate maps as yet of these inner worlds. Whilst the various types of occultist and psychologist go their diverse ways, some exploring mountains and others the valleys, and with different aims in mind, it is hardly surprising if different flora and fauna are described. On the other hand those representing the sceptical establishment tend to deny that such a land exists, whilst those of the religious orthodoxies consider it forbidden territory too dangerous to be explored.

We would simply say that as far as the ritual magician is concerned, whatever our later evaluation of their nature and validity, the important thing is to take these forms at face value, for lack of belief in them will certainly wither any possible results on the vine.

This does not necessarily mean that the images are entirely subjective, but that the tuning of our perception to another level of conscious reality through the medium of images is dependent upon our belief in them. This is what Coleridge, in regard to the related form of theatrical art, called "the willing suspension of disbelief".

As far as the magician is concerned, there is an objective reality within or behind the astral forms. Otherwise, why bother to work with them? In the record given in *Dion Fortune`s Magical Battle of Britain* we see the use of astral forms by a meditation group which seemed to key in with expressions of the general psyche of the nation at the time. The matter of coincidence, cause and effect, is a matter for later analysis and theorisation. What matters to the practising occultist is that he or she feels called upon to do it, as a combined matter of personal fulfilment and public duty.

Whether this be delusion or not is a matter for personal judgment. As a somewhat bemused reviewer of the Dion Fortune book remarked, not without truth, "this is for those who like their weird stuff straight!" In other words, it is not for fantasy fiction, it is for real. Yet much the same could be said for the matter of prayer.

In the more recent example of magical working that we have quoted, the Chapels of Remembrance and the possible existence of an inner group dedicated to this kind of work, we seem to have a kind of halfway house between magic and prayer - both utilising "astral forms".

An extract from the inner communicator of this particular piece of work seems to confirm this.

I would just like to explain how you have helped our poor friends in the chapel. This kind of meditation work is like intercessory prayer, to some extent, although it is empowered by its structural intention - it is not a vague plea but a decisive act. It also, of course, forms an energised imprint on both our planes through our mutual concentration, which helps to increase its efficacy. You have read in the channelled work of Olive Pixley [author of "The Armour of Light" "Listening In" etc., Ed], that praying for the soul of a deceased person is like sending them a present. And that is true. But let me explain it in a different way to give you a wider understanding. Imagine the Sacred Heart of Christ as being like a red-hot and glowing charcoal disc. As a Roman Catholic, the image of the Sacred Heart will be not only familiar to you but also powerfully significant, although it is a much, much deeper and more cosmically significant image even than most Catholics realise. But let's not get into that just now. Just see the Sacred Heart, the burning, compassionate centre of the Incarnate God, the hub of Tiphareth, the source of the Light of Christ, as a charcoal block. When you think compassionate thoughts, or pray, or do a meditation or ritual of this kind, it is rather like dropping incense grains onto that glowing disc. With directly proportional results - a fleeting merciful thought would be like one of those little splinters or aromatic wood that flash and vanish in a tiny and momentary puff of smoke. A full-blown ritual done with intent would be like a great big knobbly lump of frankincense, which would burn for much longer and with a much richer and more prolific smoke. Whatever your offering, the smoke is absorbed (breathed in, if you like) by God. And so you can do a lot of good for these afflicted souls by directing your charitable intentions into the Heart of Christ, from whence they may ascend in spirit to God in His Ultimate Majesty. You and I, my dear, are going to stoke up a humdinger of a bonfire with our chunks of incense, and get the Light of Christ and the Love of God positively streaming into that neglected little chapel.

Here we have an explanation of the use of astral forms as a means of communication and transition between one plane of being and another, mediating even between the depths of despair of "spirits in prison" and the heights of divine compassion. And also a practical example of the aim and *modus operandi* of one particular form of white magic.

APPENDIX C

THE HIGH CROSS TEMPLE WORKING
Gareth Knight

It seems that a book of this nature would not be complete without a full specimen ritual of the type that is performed today by at least one serving group of the Western Esoteric Tradition. This particular one was performed on the weekend of 5th/6th November 1988.

The idea for a ritual working comes to a practising magician in much the same way that a poem comes to a poet or a screen play to a dramatic writer. The only difference probably being that in the case of the magical operator, the idea may have been dropped there by an inner plane source, the result of which is for the recipient to find a certain irrational preoccupation with some particular complex of imagery or ideas. The effect is something after the fashion depicted in the popular film *Close Encounters of the Third Kind* only with not quite so dramatic a dénouement. The end result is usually some kind of magical working rather than a physical confrontation with beings from another planet!

Leafing through magical diaries and contemporary reports, 1988 seems to have been a particularly active year. At this particular time I had been getting a great deal of pressure coming through centering upon the city of London. This crystallised, so to speak, on the occasion when upon receipt of a gift from my company for 21 years service, I had to drive into the city to pick up an astronomical telescope. This somehow led to a preoccupation with Sir Christopher Wren, who started out in life as an astronomer, and who went on to become the architect for the reconstruction of London after the Great Fire of 1666.

Another member of my group was similarly affected, which led to a great deal of walking the streets of the city, and many of these are still left even if swallowed up by edifices of glass and concrete. For instance Bread Street is still there, although one looks in vain for anything more than a plaque to commemorate the old Mermaid Tavern. But in the interstices of all this the old London still stands, marked out by many of the churches designed by Wren, and which remained even after Hitler's blitzkrieg - if now somewhat dwarfed by modern high rise temples of Mammon. But it was ever thus, and Wren's original designs in his day were badly mauled by seventeenth century commercial opportunism.

Another grand idea of his that was rendered still-borne was his original design for St. Paul's Cathedral, and the great model for this, large enough for a man to stand within it, nowadays stands in the crypt. Originally plastered and gilded, bereft of its paint it is still a formidable piece of antique joinery and also of very considerable symbolic significance. If anyone were seeking for national talismans this is one indeed.

Built on a four-square design, like an equal armed cross under a central dome, it embodies many ancient magical principles. It was rejected by the ecclesiastical commissioners of the time who sought for something more along the lines of what they had been used to, a more Gothic form cathedral plan. It is recorded that Christopher Wren wept at this rejection, and vowed never to build another model for the benefit of future unimaginative clientèle.

Whether he had any conscious esoteric ideas in mind for this original design is a mute point but, perhaps deriving from contemporary masonry, one or two aspects of the detailing seem particularly esoteric, such as a statue of St. Paul, (of all people) surmounting a cubic stone on a pyramidal structure of seven steps.

Perhaps as befits a national ecclesiastical monument, which seems to have served as such on its high hill within the city limits even in Roman times as a temple of Diana, much legendary lore surrounds the building of the new structure. The most famous of which is perhaps the one that recounts how, seeking for a lump of stone to demonstrate a particular idea to the king, Wren asked a workman to pull a piece out of the rubble at random, which turned out to have the word RESURGAM engraved upon it. In more recent times the figure of Wren and his close assistant Nicholas Hawksmoor have inspired *Hawksmoor*, a powerful novel by Peter Ackroyd, who seems to have a strong, possibly unconscious, clairvoyant facility to tap into former times. Not that the novel should be taken as too close a character study of Wren and Hawksmoor but rather an evocative demonstration of some of the less salubrious psychic dynamics of certain strata of a great city and their reflections through time.

Certainly, to the esotericist, the experience of a great city is quite a powerful one in its pull on the imagination at various levels. And this indeed provokes a genre of literary reminiscence about big cities, beneath the tourist floss, that is not all jingoism and nostalgia. These are power points within the national psyche, and as productive as psychic centres as any natural object or ancient site of past religious glories. Modern travel routes, by land, sea or air are as much "ley lines" in their way, as anything dreamed up from ancient landmarks.

It may have been something in this connection that led to my being invited to New York to lecture at this time (and coincidentally the Great Model did the trip a year later!) It became apparent however that the lectures and workshops were probably the least important element of my esoteric agenda. It seemed that for some reason I was required to pace many of the older streets of New York as I had trod those of the city of London, being conscious at the same time of the parallels between the two. Financial power seemed an important part of this and in particular I felt compelled to concentrate upon Wall Street, which indeed is the street that marks the pallisade that guarded the old Dutch trading post of New Amsterdam. Whilst Broadway is the old Indian track which led down from up-state New England to this important and highly energetic focus for the future where the waters of the Hudson and East Rivers meet, in the confluence of which now stands the statue of Liberty, donated by the post-revolutionary democratic idealists of France.

At the same time my interest in Sir Christopher Wren burgeoned, which led of course to another ancient and significant site, that of Greenwich, a centre of Tudor monarchy, with all the importance that this period had for the history of the nation, the English language, and the foundation of the nation state. Here Sir Christopher Wren was commissioned to build the Royal Observatory with international scientific and cultural repercussions.

It has also been suggested that there might be an inner magical group responsible for much of this, tentatively labelled "the Fidele", and associated with contemporary figures surrounding the formation of the Royal Society, which has its magical elements as Dr. Frances Yates has expounded in *The Rosicrucian Enlightenment* and elsewhere. We would consider this to include an interest in architecture as well as theatre, of which Sir John Vanbrugh is a notable example, another of Wren's associates. All this seems to form part of a more general seventeenth century progression of which Ben Jonson's court masques with Inigo Jones seem to have set something in motion, for it would seem to be that beneath all the courtly flummery some of these masques, with actual royal persons taking part, bear many hallmarks of magical ritual with their diverse mythological themes and idealistic aspirations.

To a commonsensical, slightly cynical, rational person of the modern world much of this may sound like a rag bag of arbitrary facts spiked upon the thread of a naive patriotism redolent of Edwardian nostalgia. However, if magic is concerned with the dynamics of group consciousness then the subconscious mentation of the nation is likely to be full of archetypes of this order. It is thus the task of the committed magician to lend his or her consciousness to the realisation and harmless expression of these dynamics, which otherwise as group complexes might well find less salubrious forms of expression, with all the political fanaticism that this implies. One could put it in a more positive frame of reference than this, in that a properly conducted ritual should *transmute* ancient forces rather than simply contain them.

This was one objective of the ritual that follows, utilising the imagery of another great lover of London and an intuitive mystic, William Blake.

A magical ritual script is heavily loaded with symbolic resonances, which means that it makes for difficult reading in the ordinary light of day; but when delivered in the ambience of a magical lodge by a skilled team, the resonances will strike home into the deeper mental processes of all present, especially if they are skilled in tuning consciousness to the underlying levels of meaning.

As an aid to study of the ritual script that follows I have added notes on some of its symbolic content and technical points of its structure. In form it is quite a traditional formal and four-square format, in contrast to the more fluid and extemporary working on the Chapels of Remembrance described earlier.

The ritual has four officers, situated at the four cardinal points of the lodge, and designated East, South, West and North, with East being the Magus, or officer in charge of proceedings. The detailed significance of each office will be revealed as we progress.

The High Cross Temple Working

[EAST opens the lodge, using the symbol of the encircled cross, and in the name and power of the Son of Light to the East, Albion to the South, Jerusalem to the West, and Britannia to the North. The Archangels in the names of Luvah and Vala to the East, Tharmas and Enion to the West, Urizen and Ahania to the South, Urthona and Enitharmon to the North.]

[In the traditional form of opening Qabalistic God Names and Archangels would generally be used but in the national dynamics being used in this ritual archetypal names and powers are taken from the works of William Blake. Their significance should become more apparent as we proceed.]

EAST: We are gathered here this day to undertake the building of a four-fold temple within the heart of this land, to act as a focus for the evocation of the Son of Light, the return of Jerusalem his bride, and the reawakening of Albion and Britannia. Therefore I ask you to assist me to open the Lodge.

[This is the statement of intention for the rite, normally made by the Magus of the lodge at about this point.]

EAST: Four officers are necessary for the working of these Mysteries. Each officer represents a force, and each force is as a note in the chord of the ritual. I shall now proceed to set that chord vibrating.

[The Magus now proceeds to contact each officer in turn, establishing what it is that each one represents, by means of formal question and answer. The repetitive nature of this sequence with each officer is ritually very effective in action. In view of the importance of the Earth powers in this particular ritual the sequence of contacting runs anticlockwise starting from the North. The formal honorifics of address are traditional.]

EAST: Very honoured officer of the northern gate, what is your situation in the lodge?

NORTH: At the northern gate, most excellent adeptus.

EAST: Why so situated?

NORTH: To guard that gate.

EAST: And your duty?

NORTH: To represent the intuitive powers of Albion.

EAST: Where do those powers reside?

NORTH: In the ancient city of Eburacum, which is known today as York.

EAST: What is the symbol of your office?

NORTH: Light, that lighteth every man that cometh into the world.

EAST: Let that symbol be placed upon the altar to signify that the powers of your office are functioning in the lodge.

[NORTH takes light to altar. Returns to seat. Salute exchanged.]

[This is the commencement of the central altar being loaded with the symbols pertaining to each quarter officer. The salute, usually the flat of the right hand raised, with the associated eye contact, is a physical affirmation of the verbally expressed intention.]

EAST: Very honoured officer of the western gate, what is your situation in the lodge?

WEST: At the western gate, most excellent adeptus.

EAST: Why so situated?

WEST: To guard that gate.

EAST: And your duty?

WEST: To represent the generative powers of Albion.

EAST: Where do those powers reside?

WEST: In the ancient city of Aquae Sulis, which is known today as Bath.

EAST: What is the symbol of your office?

WEST: A block of carbon, the basis of all organic life, glowing with fire.

EAST: Let that symbol be placed upon the altar to signify
          that the powers of your office are functioning in
          the lodge.

*[WEST ignites charcoal block at altar and places it on thurible. Returns
to seat. Salute exchanged.]*

EAST: Very honoured officer of the southern gate, what is
          your situation in the lodge?
SOUTH: At the southern gate, most excellent adeptus.
EAST: Why so situated?
SOUTH: To guard that gate.
EAST: And your duty?
SOUTH: To represent the rational powers of Albion.
EAST: Where do those powers reside?
SOUTH: In the ancient city of Venta Belgarum, which is
          known today as Winchester.
EAST: What is the symbol of your office?
SOUTH: The bell, that speaks to men with the tongue
          of angels.
EAST: Let that symbol be placed upon the altar to signify
          that the powers of your office are functioning in the
          lodge.

*[SOUTH takes bell to altar. Tolls it three times, in direction once
each of west, north and east. Places it on altar. Returns to seat. Salute
exchanged.]*

EAST: The situation of the magus of this lodge is at the
          eastern gate. He represents the principle of love within
          the heart of Albion, which power is represented by the
          ancient city of Londinium Augusta, which is known
          today as London. The symbol of his office is the
          incense collected from many parts of the Earth, that
          permeates the temple with its fragrance when
          burned upon the altar of sacrifice. I shall now
          place the incense upon the fire upon the altar to

signify that the powers of my office are functioning in this lodge.

[EAST places incense in thurible. Returns to place. Salutes powers behind the east, and sits.]

EAST: By the power vested in me in another place, which is duly expressed in Earth, I now declare this lodge of the mysteries to be open. Let the brethren, visible and invisible, enter upon their duties.

[This concludes the formal opening section of the rite. The four offices have been identified and their powers invoked by means of placing their various symbols upon the altar and the verbal interchange with the Magus. The choice of symbols, including that of the towns, is to a large extent arbitrary, although with a certain internal intuitive logic at the choice and discretion of the writer. This follows on the custom of William Blake whose use of symbolism was somewhat idiosyncratic but none the worse for that. If one goes along with it, rather than cavilling over possible alternatives, it works well enough. The essence of practical magic is "being of one mind in one place" even if elements of symbolic detail could legitimately be open to discussion outside the lodge.

The main drift of the symbolism has been the identifying of certain attributes of the giant Albion, who in Blake's mythology particularly, represents, at least in part, the group soul of the land of Britain. The use of ancient names is a device to stimulate the historical and legendary imagination and emotions of participants.

The final salute to the east by the Magus and his final injunction is an overt reminder that a magical ritual is a co-operative act between those on the outer and those on the inner planes.

We now proceed to the sequence which is technically known as the Composition of Mood or Composition of Place.

Mood will already have been established to a certain degree by what has gone before, but now we home in upon a specific imaginative location that fine-tunes consciousness to the purpose of the rite.]

EAST: Let the very honoured officer of the northern gate, representing the forces of the higher wisdom within this lodge, lead us to the site of the secret inner temple within the heart of Albion.

NORTH: I invite you to come with me upon a journey. Therefore close your eyes, and sinking deeply into meditation, visualise the scenes described. We are floating over the land of Albion, which we see stretched out below us like a deep purple shadow under the night sky. About its shores the waves of the sea can be discerned, glittering silver in the starlight.

We see the outline of the coast, that which has been called Merlin's Enclosure. We see it stretching from Lindisfarne, the Holy Island in the north east, down the Yorkshire coast, past the Fens and the Wash, and around the curve of East Anglia. From the inlet of the River Thames it turns the corner of the coast of Kent. We see the white cliffs that extend along the channel coast until they give way to the ancient rock peninsula of the far south west. Around Land's End the coast continues across the Severn estuary to encompass the mighty rocks of the Principality of Wales. Then past the lake and hill and dale it goes until the western end of the great wall is reached. We pass in vision along the forts and encampments along the wall until the circuit is completed along the great wall.

We see the four great cities that are represented at the four quarters of our lodge. They stand as four-square patterns of light. We see also the great rivers of the land. The Thames in the east. The Solent in the south. The Severn in the west. The Humber in the north. And many others beside that form a web of veins and arteries, and outline the lineaments of the body of earth and rock that is formed by the hills and valleys of Albion.

We see the Roman roads, the rectilinear outlines of the principle of law and order in a mighty empire. We also see the less structured serpentine tracery of the hill fires of the tribes, their trackways and their tribal capitals.

Albion in the time of Rome is a tempered balance between the ordered empire and the natural wild. It is also the far western outpost of the world, that holds within it dreams of an ancient past and a distant future, that are its special destiny to cherish and preserve. Of Atlantis in the past of linear time; and of America in the future.

But our purpose this day is to journey to the centre of all these powers, and so we gently descend through the air, toward the surface of the land. We see as we do so two great road ways below us, one Roman, one native. Where they cross they cut the land into four quarters, so it is as if we approach the centre of a circled cross.

From south east to north west runs the great Roman road of Watling Street, joining the ports of the coast of Kent to the fastnesses of northern Wales and the Druid island of Mona. From south west to north east runs the great ancient track of the tribes that is called the Fosse Way. It runs from the tin mines of the Cornish peninsula up to Lincoln and the Great North Road that leads to the fortresses of the Great Wall and the unconquered tribes. Where the two ways intersect is our present destination. No city known to man stands there, but it is simply known as the High Cross.

Our feet touch the soft springy grass of the high heath land and we march in silence, under the stars, towards where the great roads cross. As we approach we are aware of the stars above our heads, and we are guided towards our destination by the shining stationary star Polaris, about which all the heavens revolve.

In the darkness ahead we see a deeper shadow. It is the sacred building towards which our footsteps are set. It is in the form of an equal armed cross. Within its centre is a massive tower capped with a great dome. And rising from the dome there is a tall and elegant steeple with bell and lantern tower. From its pinnacle there shines a silver light that is like an earthly counter-part of the Polar Star above us.

[This has been a very pictorial passage for the express reason of allowing all present to build the images within their imagination. According to magical theory their imagination becomes to a large extent the imagination, an inner objective state shared by all those present, "visible or invisible"

The frontiers of the chosen area of land have been drawn from the particular point in time when the Roman empire ruled over the Celtic tribes, this being a popular traditional image and thus imaginatively effective, and no considerations of a contemporary political nature entered into this choice. One has to draw the line somewhere, as the saying goes, and this in the circumstances of the ritual seemed the most appropriate.

More symbolically important are the images of balance between opposites - between Roman imperial civilisation and the native culture of the tribes, pointed up by the two roads representative of the two cultures, which also serve to make a patterned quaternio of the land considered as magic circle. The central point, High Cross, does actually exist on the map to this day, as do the two roads, duly tarmacadamed. The Roman road Watling Street is the main trunk road known as the A5, and the Fosse Way is a minor road running up from Stretton-under-Fosse. A rather dilapidated 18th century monument marks the spot of High Cross, traditionally regarded as the centre of England. Apart from that there is little, save a guest house and a tall radio mast.

Another important symbolic dimension included in this passage is the reference to the Pole Star, which although it may be but one small star in a large galaxy is particularly important to the Earth, at any rate in its present epoch, as approximately marking the axis of the planet's spin. It thus represents an important symbolic magical direction, in addition to the terrestrial ones of the four quarters. As we shall later see, a further important direction is down into the centre of the Earth, whilst between all six directions is the High Cross itself, upon which we are about to evoke an inner edifice, already seen in outline and marked by a star-like light. Having been brought thus far by the northern officer the magus now takes over to introduce us to the symbolic inner guides who will introduce us in more detail to this inner edifice, or "temple not built with hands".]

EAST: As we approach we are intercepted by an old man carrying a serpent staff. He steps out from the shadows as if from nowhere. It is the arch-mage Merlin, the guardian of these mysteries. His eyes glitter in the star light as he intently scans the face of each one of us.

[PAUSE]

Satisfied with his inspection, he turns and leads the way towards the western arm of the building. Here, he strikes with his staff upon the great doorway. The door is flung open and we stand in a blaze of light.

Another custodian is there to welcome us. He beckons us in. Merlin remains outside to guard his enclosure, and we see that we are in the hands of a latter day counterpart, the prophet Blake. This is the first of many transformations that we may see in this holy place.

We contemplate its structure. All four cities represented in our outer lodge have their link with it. A model of its actual form is to this day kept within the city of Londinium Augusta. For when the astronomer and architect Christopher Wren designed a new cathedral to replace the one that had been destroyed by fire his inspiration came from within the sacred archives of this land and the guardians who watch over it. There his first model, rejected by those who were dim in interior vision, still stands. There, in the crypt of the new building, it broods like a seed within the husk of the cathedral of St. Paul, or like a germ within the egg.

SOUTH: At the centre of our temple, the equal arms of the cross intersect beneath the tower and dome. There we see a circle upon which no man dares to tread. This central circle is the prototype of the Table Round, that was the dowry of Queen Guenevere, given to her father by the arch-mage Merlin. A model of this Table Round is to be seen to this day upon the wall of the halls of rulership and law within the city of Venta Belgarum. And about this form all can meet in equality and freedom under the law. And many of the outer world come to it in pilgrimage each day.

WEST: As we gaze more closely upon that central circle we see why no man stands upon it. It is composed of another element, a sheet of water, from which wisps of vapour rise. It is indeed another form of the ancient Cauldron of Inspiration and the quality of its healing and magical waters may be witnessed to this day in the springs and baths of the city of Aquae Sulis, to which all may come to be cleansed and healed, and the wise to seek wisdom.

NORTH: Above the circle of the pool the tower rises with bells and beacon, high over the dome. This is the link with the northern city of Eburacum, a city famed for towers, from the Roman multi-angular tower of William the Norman, once of wood, which also still stands. And here in latter days the lightning struck tower of the minster gave witness and warning to those who lack or abandon belief in the power of the higher forces.

[In this section we have been introduced to a guide, a conscious intelligent being, as introductor to that which is to follow. The identifications used are in terms of function or archetype, rather than personal, even though such guides are capable of acting on occasion in a very personal and intelligent way, perhaps when ensouled by an inner plane being acting in much the same way as a physical plane lodge officer identifies with a ritual office. Thus we are not necessarily invoking the personality of William Blake in the mode of a spiritualist séance but rather the prophetic principle that he stood for and embodied whilst in life. The same goes for the more legendary and temporally remote Merlin.

The references to the towns previously invoked in the opening are a demonstration of the interweaving of symbolic resonances in any effective magical working. Much of what is described has its physical plane counterpart, which serves also to "earth" the powers of the ritual at least in the minds of those present. As for instance the replica of the Round Table that hangs in the municipal buildings at Winchester, even though of course it is but a medieval replica, one of many fashionable in its day, and later used for target practice in less mythopoeically appreciative Cromwellian days. Similarly, in relation to York, any popular tradition may be incorporated to add to the magically emotive "weight", such as the belief amongst some that the tower of York Minster was struck by lightning in connection with the ordination of the Bishop of Durham, an academically inclined ecclesiastic who cast doubt upon some of the traditional tenets of the Christian faith.

The intention in all of this symbolism is to be selective according to the immediate object in hand. This may very well seem illogical and arbitrary at the level of the analytical conscious intellect but we are dealing with a deeper level of intuitive and subliminal relationships in magical work. Thus magical work **is** "all imagination", but no responsible magician claimed it was anything else!.

The immediate magical objective has been to link the powers of the four quarters of the lodge with the central inner plane edifice being built. This in turn is linked imaginatively with the centre of the land and with the remarkable design of Sir Christopher Wren's earlier design for St. Paul's cathedral than that which was ultimately built; a design which in its four square structure had many magical resonances, whether Sir Christopher realised that fact or not.

The next phase of the ritual aims to link the symbolism to the traditions of the main races that occupied the land in the course of history, rather like the strata of a psychic archaeological dig.]

EAST: We who stand at the level of the four great halls of nave and transept about the central circle, now invoke the assistance of our ancestors. Upon the level upon which we stand are assembled about us all the peoples that share with us the common heritage of Albion.

EAST: In the eastern arm we salute the Angles and the Saxons.

NORTH: In the northern arm we salute the Vikings and the Danes.

SOUTH: In the southern arm we salute the Romans and the Normans.

WEST: In the western arm we salute the Celts and the Britons.

EAST: We feel and acknowledge the power of all these peoples around the central focus of the temple, and all individuals and small groups of other races, throughout all time, who have come in law and love, in refuge or in strength, to join us in Merlin's Enclosure.

[We now proceed to link in four elements of genius pertaining to the national consciousness as a whole, using once more as a device a particular character chosen from popular history as an archetypal focus as an aid to the imagination. Again, we are not calling up the personalities of departed celebrities - simply the ambience of the charisma that has become attached to their roles in the national life. Nonetheless the physical plane officers present may well feel a strong overshadowing that may seem to all intents and purposes very much like taking on the character and dress of the figure invoked. This can happen with completely legendary or even fictional characters, and is a psychological process that seems to have something in common with "method" acting.]

EAST: At each of the four quarters about the central circle there is a high throne. At each of these sits a human Grand Master. Those who at present sit within these places are those who embody a particular principle and who were incarnate at the beginning of the modern age. Let us invoke the presence and powers of these four Grand Masters.

In the Eastern throne sits the regal figure of Charles, the second king of that name. All royal figures of Albion carry an archetypal principle upon their human shoulders. In the case of the second Charles it is that of the Restored King. He is also a king renouned for his great loves, not only of women but of his people amongst whom he mingled as the city burned. He who was protected as a young man in the Royal Oak against the forces of insurrection. And who restored the Roman image of Britannia to the coinage of the realm, with one whom he loved as the model. He who also was patron of arts and sciences, founder of the Royal Society, and the restorer of the magic of the stage.

WEST: In the western throne there sits a commoner, Samuel Pepys. One who so loved the world that he wrote within a journal the whole of life about him. Who was the loyal servant of his king and country, as maker and breaker of secret codes in defence against unknown enemies, and secretary of the navy, upon which, from the time of Alfred the Great, through Henry Tudor and Elizabeth, to his own time and thereafter, there rested the power and trade and defence of Britannia and her genius for exploration.

SOUTH: In the southern throne there sits one who calculated and measured the very heavens, even Sir Isaac Newton. He whose towering intellect, questing uncharted seas of thought, discovered the very force that binds and rules the movement of the heavenly bodies within the starry sky. He whose researches embraced the sum of human knowledge, from alchemy to bible history, from calculus to the quality of light, and who as Master of the Royal Mint ruled over the smelting of the coin of the realm.

NORTH: In the northern throne there sits one who started life as an astronomer but whose lasting monument is in the buildings that still grace our land, even Sir Christopher Wren. He who rebuilt the capital after the years of pestilence and fire, and set up the glory of the spires within it, that still hold high their heads beneath the towers of corporate greed. And maintaining a talismanic link with sea and stars built the Naval Hospital and the Royal Observatory at Greenwich from whence is measured the longitudes of the whole Earth for the guidance of all mariners and those who fly the skies.

[Much the same dynamics apply in the invocations of the Grand Masters as applied in those of the four cities. One has a

potted biography looking at the very best and inspirational as a paradigm for national aspiration. Thus the brightest possible light is shone upon Charles II's sexual proclivities against which, in real life, he was nicknamed Old Rowley after one of his racing stallions at Newmarket. Also the opportunity is taken to link in a reference to Britannia, which is one of the Blakean archetypes that we shall shortly be dealing with. Similarly the less admirable sides of any of the other personalities are ignored, which is not so much a matter of hypocrisy or fastidiousness as magical hygiene and focus of spiritual intention.

We now pass to making the link with these qualities, valid in the history of the nation, with the archetypal figures that feature in William Blake's poetic mythology, the Four Zoas and their Emanations.

During this sequence all present will be actively imagining the scenes described upon the interior of the dome above which, if the rite is working properly, with inner plane co-operation, will seem to be very much alive and imaginatively inter-active with the beholders.]

EAST: King Charles speaks from the power point of the eastern throne. "Look up to the dome above. There you will see depicted the Holy Living Creatures associated with our land, the Four Zoas and their Emanations of the prophet Blake. Regard the eastern quarter of the dome. There see Luvah, the wine grower, the prince of love, and with him his beloved one, called Vala. See their pictures upon the dome begin to burst forth into actual angelic life, standing in the midst of a scene of Bacchic revelry and joyful harvest in the vinyards."

WEST: Samuel Pepys speaks from the power point of the western throne. "Look up at the dome above. There see within the western quarter the Zoa Tharmas, the shepherd and navigator upon the waters, with his beloved one, called Enion. See their pictures upon the dome begin to burst forth into life, standing in the midst of a pastoral idyll of nymphs and shepherds and fishermen in small boats amongst the sporting dolphins and mermaids and other friendly creatures of the deep."

SOUTH: Sir Isaac Newton speaks from the power point of the southern throne. "Look up at the dome above. There see within the southern quarter the Zoa Urizen, the prince of light, driver of the plough team and framer of laws, together with his beloved one, called Ahania. See them in the midst of the ploughed and tilled fields of a busy farmstead, amidst the cultivators and husbandmen of the land."

NORTH: Sir Christopher Wren speaks from the power point of the northern throne. "Look up to the dome above. There see within the northern quarter the Zoa Urthona, the smith, the maker of artefacts, together with his beloved one, called Enitharmon. See them at the forge of a village smithy, beside the duck pond and the green, beneath a spreading chestnut tree, shoeing the great dray horses, and forging the metal implements of rural life".

[And now commences a deepening of the level of the work as the reflection of these ideals is evoked from within the depths of the pool below, within which, in psychological terms, lies the deep unconscious collective mind of the nation. This is of course a magical extension upon that of Wren's "great model" insofar that he made no provision for a central circular pool and well, an under-earth reflection of the structure that rises above! Although it has to be said that the crypt in the actual building is quite a powerful place, as may be discerned by anyone who stands with any degree of sensitivity upon the brass grill in the floor that lies above it, directly under the centre of the great dome and high spire.]

EAST: From the heights of the dome above the Holy Living Creature Luvah speaks. "Look into the waters of the pool beneath. See what floats before your vision. And deep down, towards the eastern side, you may see a glowing head. It is that of Bran the Blessed, which was buried at the White Mount, at the eastern wall of Londinium Augusta."

WEST: From the heights of the dome above the Holy Living Creature Tharmas speaks. "Look into the waters of the pool beneath. See what floats befor your vision. And deep down, towards the western side, you may see a glowing head. It is that of Sulis, that graced the pediment of the temple and holy springs of Sulis Minerva in the midst of the city of Aquae Sulis."

SOUTH: From the heights of the dome above the Holy Living Creature Urizen speaks. "Look into the waters of the pool beneath. See what floats before your vision. And deep down, towards the southern side, you may see a glowing head. It is that of Orpheus, the tamer of wild beasts, who safely passed into and out of the Underworld. He whose temples were spread throughout this land and even to this day are to be found in four fold mosaic at Littlecote, in the southern realms whose ancient capital was Venta Belgarum."

NORTH: From the heights of the dome above the Holy Living Creature Urthona speaks. "Look into the waters of the pool beneath. See what floats before your vision as you gaze into the waters. And deep down, towards the northern side, you may see a glowing head. It is that of Mithras, surrounded by a lion's mane and aureole of light. Even he who followed the armies and marched with the legions, whose banners were safeguarded in the temple in the city of Eburacum."

EAST: As we become aware of the powers of the four mystic heads, our vision deepens, and penetrates the very depths of the pool of inspiration.

       In the deep centre of the pool between the four is a shaft that plunges deep into the Earth. Our vision strives to penetrate its depths. There we can just discern the gleaming of a point of light, as if it were a distant star.

       We are also aware that this deepest point within the centre of the pool contains a reflection of the dome and hollow tower above. However, it is not a mere reflection, but is also vibrant with its own life. Thus we see an interchange between the deep well, within whose depths we see the distant star within the centre of the Earth, and the tower above, whose hollow tube acts like a well, as a channel for the light of the star of the northern pole.

WEST: Now we begin to see a stirring within the very depths, as of some deep-sea creature whose den is down within that primeval shaft toward the centre of the Earth. It is the circling movement of a mighty dragon, coiled round the mouth of the pit.

       We also see, superimposed upon the vision in the depths, the reflection of the stars above, as if the dome above our heads had become as clear as crystal to allow the passage of the light. And all along the dragon's back within the depths we see the lights of the stars of the constellation Draco, that coils about the northern pole.

SOUTH: And now within the depths of the pool, we see a dark and cumbrous figure emerging from the central shaft. At first sight quite small, it grows in size, and then begins to swim in circles round about the encircled form of the dragon. We see it is a bear.

Reflected like shining diamond points within its dark fur we also see the pattern of the stars that form the Great Bear. Slowly we see the bear begin to rise. As it spirals towards the surface so does it undergo a transformation, and take on the form of a young woman. We recall that the Great Bear in origin was said to be the beautiful nymph Callisto.

EAST: The interaction of the worlds is such that we find it difficult to determine that which comes from above and that which comes from below. Suffice to say that there now stands, within the centre of the pool before us, a radiant figure who seems to partake of both, and whose beauty dazzles the eye.

NORTH: But we are bidden to return our eyes of vision down once more into the depths of the pool. There we see a further mystery. A giant form now circles within the depths, as of a mighty man. He also begins to rise toward the surface, and as he spirals upward so we realise that he too is outlined with stars that we know in the northern sky as Bootes, the Bear Herd. And at the creative centre of his body there shines the brilliant star Arcturus.

EAST: Again we can hardly determine that which comes from above and that which comes from below. But now before us in the centre of the temple there also stands a mighty god-like giant.

And so we see before us, two great magical forms that were known in the annals of the Qabalistic wisdom as the naked man, very strong, he who stands at the Foundation of the Kingdom. And also of the beautiful naked woman, the morning and evening star of seven rayed beauty, the first and last perfection of creation, the feminine exemplar of the Sphere of Venus.

As we gaze upon them we realise they are known by other names, and ones that strike upon our very being and our destiny. For they are those mighty beings described by the prophet Blake, the Giant Albion and the Heavenly Jerusalem.

A bright and blinding light begins to build between the forms of Albion and Jerusalem, as if a coalescing of their stars. And before our eyes there grows from them a child. A miraculously transforming child. At first it is a babe within their arms. But then they set him down before them, and he begins to crawl, and then to walk, in a blaze of light, walking upon the waters in a spiral way, that glows with phosphorescent light where his feet have trod. He himself is aflame with brilliant light. And as he goes upon his spiral way he starts to dance and spin and twirl and laugh for joy and delight, and growing older as he does so, from boy to youth, from youth to young man.

And now he stands at the easternmost point of the circumference of the circular pool and holds out his hands towards the couple in the centre. As he does so, a tranformation begins to occur within the body of Jerusalem, for she is the chosen one to be the Bride of the Son of Light. But by the laws of heaven, her lover the giant Albion shall not be degraded or deprived, for from within the body and soul of Jerusalem a sister emanates that shall be the bride of Albion.

And so the four figures of light now take up their stations.

[This is the climax of the rite, with the four figures that play a major part in the mythology of William Blake being finally evoked, with resonances of magical images from the Tree of Life

of the Qabalah, as channels and lenses of divine power into the astral ethers beyond the immediate confines of the lodge.]

EAST: All hail, the Son of Light, who stands within the East.

WEST: All hail, Jerusalem his Bride, who stands within the West.

SOUTH: All hail, the giant Albion, who stands within the South.

NORTH: All hail, Britannia his Bride, who stands within the North.

EAST: The four figures turn and face outward. The Grand Masters on their thrones, the Holy Living Creatures in the dome, the assembled nations at the four quarters of the temple, turn outward as well.

So let the forces of this lodge ray forth through all the realms of the land and the Earth

O Divine Saviour, arise upon the mountains of Albion, as in ancient time. Behold, the cities of Albion seek thy face. And then Jesus appeared, standing by Albion as the Good Shepherd by the lost sheep that he hath found. And Albion knew that it was the Lord, the Universal Humanity. And Albion saw his form, a man, and they conversed as man to man in ages of eternity.

WEST: Awake, awake, Jerusalem. O lovely Emanation of Albion, awake and overspread all nations as in ancient time. For lo, the night of death is past, and the Eternal Day appears upon our hills. Awake Jerusalem, and come away.

SOUTH: The Four Living Creatures, Chariots of Humanity, Divine, incomprehensible, in beautiful Paradise expand. These are the four rivers of Paradise and the four faces of Humanity, fronting the four cardinal points of Heaven, going forward, forward, irresistibly, from eternity to eternity.

NORTH: England awake! Awake! Awake! Jerusalem thy sister calls. Why wilt thou sleep the sleep of death and close her from thy ancient walls? The Breath Divine breathed over Albion, and England, who is Britannia, awoke from death on Albion's bosom.

And I beheld London, a human aweful wonder of God, saying "Return Albion, return. I give myself for thee. My streets are my ideas of my imagination. Awake Albion awake. And let us wake together. My houses are thoughts, my inhabitants affections; the children of my thoughts walking within my blood vessels. For Albion's sake and for Jerusalem his Emanation, I give myself, and these my brothers give themselves for Albion."

So spoke London, immortal guardian. I see thee, aweful parent land, in light. Behold I see London, Bath, Winchester and York, venerable parents of men, generous immortal guardians, golden clad. For cities are men, fathers of multitudes. And rivers and mountains are also men. Everything is human, mighty and sublime. In every bosom a universe expands, as wings let down at will around, and called the Universal Tent.

EAST: To mercy, pity, peace and love, all pray in their distress. And to these virtues of delight, return their thankfulness.

For mercy, pity, peace and love is God, our father dear. And mercy, pity, peace and love is man, his child and care.

For mercy has a human heart; pity, a human face. And love the human form divine; and peace the human dress. Then every man of every clime, that prays in his distress. Prays to the human form divine - love, mercy, pity, peace.

And all must love the human form, in heathen, Turk or Jew. Where mercy, love and pity dwell, there God is dwelling too.

Let us for a short space before we leave this hallowed place, mediate the healing forces within this lodge to all within the planetary sphere of Earth. Especially to all in need, in sorrow, in torment, in error, or in danger. Be they human or angel, animal or elemental, incarnate or discarnate. To all that fall may the Lord bring swift deliverance.

Come says the spirit. Come says the bride. Come let each hearer reply.

Come forward you who are thirsty, accept the waters of life.

[After due pause and allowing for any impromptu statement or working, EAST closes in the same formula as was the opening.]

*   *   *   *   *

As far as rituals go this is not one of the easiest to perform, or even to understand, and it may thus perhaps seem a little out of place in a text that purports to be an *introduction* to ritual. Nonetheless there is little point in starting out on a journey if one has little idea where it might end.

To the untutored eye a cursory glance through the script might glean nothing more than what appear to be obscure abstractions couched in overblown language. However, to experience the ritual in performance by experienced practitioners can be a different thing altogether - with the proviso that has been mentioned earlier that to a completely untrained outsider there is little instruction or entertainment in sitting in on a magical ritual.

This applies to journalists, academics and interested friends and relatives alike. It is not for nothing that magic is classified as "esoteric" - for the few. But then much the same could be said of other vehicles that demand some measure of dedication and discernment in any of the arts and sciences.

Much of the higher magical elements in the above script are from the pen of William Blake, and therefore much depends upon one's appreciation of the aims and climax of the ritual as to whether one regards Blake as an ancient eccentric penning unintelligible ravings, or an inspired prophet speaking poetically of higher things in the simplest and most direct way that is verbally possible.

This working is certainly less accessible to immediate conscious understanding than the Chapel of Remembrance working, but forms part of the rich and varied patterns of magical expression that may be utilised by the modern ritual magician. It will be apparent that much of the work we have described concerns national dynamics rather than a more universalist aspect. This however is of the nature of magical as of psychological work. Our immediate concerns must lie in the balance of our personal selves, without which we cannot form meaningful social or familial relationships. Beyond the family comes the group, be it in terms of race or nation, and in this respect we look upon the world as a family of nations, not an abstract humanity devoid of any individual personality or diverse cultural traditions. We have shown what can be done within terms of our own symbolic back yard, it remains for students of other cultures and countries to make their own adaptations using their own traditions and symbolic resonances.

This is specialised work, and as in any other discipline, cannot always be described in words of one syllable or made to add up in terms of simple arithmetic. However, if nothing else, we publish this material in the hope that it will go some way to show that there is rather more to magic than wish fulfilment conjurations in search of personal love or fortune, or the sinister associations that are largely the projection of the shadow side of enthusiastic religious fundamentalists, or indeed the colourful speculations of popular entertainment that are as accurate as the average detective novel is to normal work of a policeman on the beat.

INDEX

Other titles from Thoth Publications

THE CIRCUIT OF FORCE
by Dion Fortune.
With commentaries by Gareth Knight.

In "The Circuit of Force", Dion Fortune describes techniques for raising the personal magnetic forces within the human aura and their control and direction in magic and in life, which she regards as 'the Lost Secrets of the Western Esoteric Tradition'.

To recover these secrets she turns to three sources.

a) the Eastern Tradition of Hatha Yoga and Tantra and their teaching on raising the "sleeping serpent power" or kundalini;

b) the circle working by means of which spiritualist seances concentrate power for the manifestation of some of their results;

c) the linking up of cosmic and earth energies by means of the structured symbol patterns of the Qabalistic Tree of Life.

Originally produced for the instruction of members of her group, this is the first time that this material has been published for the general public in volume form.

Gareth Knight provides subject commentaries on various aspects of the etheric vehicle, filling in some of the practical details and implications that she left unsaid in the more secretive esoteric climate of the times in which she wrote.

Some quotes from Dion Fortune's text:

"When, in order to concentrate exclusively on God, we cut ourselves off from nature, we destroy our own roots. There must be in us a circuit between heaven and earth, not a one-way flow, draining us of all vitality. It is not enough that we draw up the Kundalini from the base of the spine; we must also draw down the divine light through the Thousand-Petalled Lotus. Equally, it is not enough for our mental health and spiritual development that we draw down the Divine Light, we must also draw up the earth forces. Only too often mental health is sacrificed to spiritual development through ignorance of, or denial of, this fact."

"....the clue to all these Mysteries is to be sought in the Tree of Life. Understand the significance of the Tree; arrange the symbols you are working with in the correct manner upon it, and all is clear and you can work out your sum. Equate the Danda with the Central Pillar, and the Lotuses with the Sephiroth and the bi-sections of the Paths thereon, and you have the necessary bilingual dictionary at your disposal - if you know how to use it."

ISBN 978-1-870450-28-7

PRINCIPLES OF HERMETIC PHILOSOPHY
By Dion Fortune & Gareth Knight

Principles of Hermetic Philosophy was the last known work written by Dion Fortune. It appeared in her Monthly letters to members and associates of the Society of the Inner Light between November 1942 and March 1944.

Her intention in this work is summed up in her own words: "The observations in these pages are an attempt to gather together the fragments of a forgotten wisdom and explain and expand them in the light of personal observation."

She was uniquely equipped to make highly significant personal observations in these matters as one of the leading practical occultists of her time. What is more, in these later works she feels less constrained by traditions of occult secrecy and takes an altogether more practical approach than in her earlier, well known textbooks.

Gareth Knight takes the opportunity to amplify her explanations and practical exercises with a series of full page illustrations, and provides a commentary on her work

ISBN 978-1-870450-34-8

*　　　*　　　*　　　*　　　*

THE STORY OF DION FORTUNE
As told to Charles Fielding and Carr Collins.

Dion Fortune and Aleister Crowley stand as the twentieth century's most influential leaders of the Western Esoteric Tradition. They were very different in their backgrounds, scholarship and style.

But, for many, Dion Fortune is the chosen exemplar of the Tradition - with no drugs, no homosexuality and no kinks. This book tells of her formative years and of her development.

At the end, she remains a complex and enigmatic figure, who can only be understood in the light of the system she evolved and worked to great effect.

There can be no definitive "Story of Dion Fortune". This book must remain incomplete. However, readers may find themselves led into an experience of initiation as envisaged by this fearless and dedicated woman.

ISBN 978-1-879450-33-1

PRACTICAL OCCULTISM
By Dion Fortune supplemented by Gareth Knight

This book contains the complete text of Dion Fortune's *Practical Occultism in Dialy Life* which she wrote to explain, simply and practically, enough of the occult doctrines and methods to enable any reasonably intelligent and well balanced person to make practical use of them in the circumstances of daily life. She gives sound advice on remembering past incarntions, working out karma, disination, the use and abuse of mind power and much more.

Gareth Knight has delved into the Dion Fortune archive to provide additional material not available before outside Dion Fortune's immediate circle. It includes instruction on astral magic, the discipline of the mysteries, inner plane communicators, black magic and mental trespassing, nature contracts and elemental shrines.

In addition, Dion Fortune's review of *The Literature of Illuminism* describes the books she found most useful in her own quest, ranging from books for beginners to those on initiation, Qabalah, occult fiction, the old gods of England, Atlantis, wirchcraft and yoga. In conclusion there is an interpretation by Dion Fortune's close friend Netta Fornario of *The Immortal Hour*, that haunting work of faery magic by Fiona Macleod, first performed at Glastonbury.

ISBN 978-1-870450-47-8

PRINCIPLES OF ESOTERIC HEALING
By Dion Fortune. Edited and arranged by Gareth Knight

One of the early ambitions of Dion Fortune along with her husband Dr Thomas Penry Evans was to found a clinic devoted to esoteric medicine, along the lines that she had fictionally described in her series of short stories *The Secrets of Dr. Taverner*. The original Dr. Taverner was her first occult teacher Dr. Theodore Moriarty, about whom she later wrote: "if there had been no Dr. Taverner there would have been no Dion Fortune!"

Shortly after their marriage in 1927 she and Dr. Evans began to receive a series of inner communications from a contact whom they referred to as the Master of Medicine. Owing to the pressure of all their other work in founding an occult school the clinic never came to fruition as first intended, but a mass of material was gathered in the course of their little publicised healing work, which combined esoteric knowledge and practice with professional medical expertise.

Most of this material has since been recovered from scattered files and reveals a fascinating approach to esoteric healing, taking into account the whole human being. Health problems are examined in terms of their physical, etheric, astral, mental or spiritual origination, along with principles of esoteric diagnosis based upon the structure of the Qabalistic Tree of Life. The function and malfunction of the psychic centres are described along with principles for their treatment by conventional or alternative therapeutic methods, with particular attention paid to the aura and the etheric double. Apart from its application to the healing arts much of the material is of wider interest for it demonstrates techniques for general development of the psychic and intuitive faculties apart from their more specialised use in assisting diagnosis.

ISBN 978-1-870450-85-0

THE SHINING PATHS

by Dolores Ashcroft-Nowicki

An Experiential Journey through the Tree of Life.

A unique collection of magical pathworkings based on the thirty-two paths of the Qabalistic Tree of Life.

Since it was first published *The Shining Paths* has become a classic of its kind, and an invaluable aid for both students and teachers.

Pathworking is the old name for what are now known as Guided Meditations. They are specifically designed visualisations into which the mind-self is projected into an inner world of learning events and situations which with training can become a complete sensory experience.

Dolores Ashcroft-Nowicki is one of the best known and most respected of contemporary Western occultists. In this book she offers a unique collection of pathworkings based on the Qabalistic Tree of Life. Each working is preceded by a discussion on the correspondences, experiences, and symbology of that path.

Dolores Ashcroft-Nowicki is a third generation psychic sensitive and a symbiotic channeller, she has worked with magic since childhood. A student of the late W.E.Butler, she was one of the Founders of The Servants of the Light School of Occult Science, of which she is now the Director of Studies. She travels the world extensively lecturing and teaching on all aspects of occultism, bringing to her students the accumulated knowledge of over half a century of study and practice.

ISBN 978-1-870450-30-0

SPIRITUALISM AND OCCULTISM

By Dion Fortune with commentary edited by Gareth Knight

As well as being an occultist of the first rank, Dion Fortune was an accomplished medium. Thus she is able to explain the methods, technicalities and practical problems of trance mediumship from first hand experience. She describes exactly what it feels like to go into trance and the different types of being one may meet with beyond the usual spirit guides.

For most of her life her mediumistic abilities were known only to her immediate circle until, in the war years, she responded to the call to try to make a united front of occultists and spiritualists against the forces of materialism in the post-war world. At this point she wrote various articles for the spiritualist press and appeared as a speaker on several spiritualist platforms

This book contains her original work *Spiritualism in the Light of Occult Science* with commentaries by Gareth Knight that quote extensively from now largely unobtainable material that she wrote on the subject during her life, including transcripts from her own trance work and rare articles from old magazines and journals.

This book represents the fourth collaborative work between the two, *An Introduction to Ritual Magic, The Circuit of Force,* and *Principles of Hermetic Philosophy* being already published in this series.

ISBN 978-1-870450-38-6

PYTHONESS The Life & Work of Margaret Lumley Brown
By Gareth Knight

Margaret Lumley Brown was a leading member of Dion Fortune's Society of the Inner Light, taking over many of Dion Fortune's functions after the latter's death in 1946. She raised the arts of seership to an entirely new level and has been hailed with some justification as the finest medium and psychic of the 20th century. Although she generally sought anonymity in her lifetime her work was the source of much of the inner teachings of the Society from 1946 to 1961 and provided much of the material for Gareth Knight's *The Secret Tradition in Arthurian Legend* and *A Practical Guide to Qabalistic Symbolism.*

Gathered here is a four part record of the life and work of this remarkable woman. Part One presents the main biographical details largely as revealed by herself in an early work *Both Sides of the Door* an account of the frightening way in which her natural psychism developed as a consequence of experimenting with an ouija board in a haunted house. Part Two consists of articles written by her on such subjects as Dreams, Elementals, the Faery Kingdom, Healing and Atlantis, most of them commissioned for the legendary but short lived magazine *New Dimensions.* Part Three provides examples of her mediumship as Archpytheness of her occult fraternity with trance addresses on topics as diverse as Elemental Contacts, Angels and Archangels, Greek and Egyptian gods, and the Holy Grail. Part Four is devoted to the occult side of poetry, with some examples of her own work which was widely published in her day.

Gareth Knight was a colleague and friend of Margaret Lumley Brown in their days in the Society of the Inner Light together, to whom in later years she vouchsafed her literary remains, some esoteric memorabilia, and the privilege of being her literary executor.

ISBN 978-1-670450-75-1

DION FORTUNE AND THE INNER LIGHT
By Gareth Knight

At last – a comprehensive biography of Dion Fortune based upon the archives of the Society of the Inner Light. As a result much comes to light that has never before been revealed. This includes:
Her early experiments in trance mediumship with her Golden Dawn teacher Maiya Curtis-Webb and in Glastonbury with Frederick Bligh Bond, famous for his psychic investigations of Glastonbury Abbey.

The circumstances of her first contact with the Masters and reception of "The Cosmic Doctrine". The ambitious plans of the Master of Medicine and the projected esoteric clinic with her husband in the role of Dr. Taverner.

The inside story of the confrontation between the Christian Mystic Lodge of the Theosophical Society of which she was president, and Bishop Piggot of the Liberal Catholic church, over the Star in the East movement and Krishnamurti. Also her group's experience of the magical conflict with Moina MacGregor Mathers.

How she and her husband befriended the young Israel Regardie, were present at his initiation into the Hermes Temple of the Stella Matutina, and suffered a second ejection from the Golden Dawn on his subsequent falling out with it.

Her renewed and highly secret contact with her old Golden Dawn teacher Maiya Tranchell-Hayes and their development of the esoteric side of the Arthurian legends.

Her peculiar and hitherto unknown work in policing the occult jurisdiction of the Master for whom she worked which brought her into unlikely contact with occultists such as Aleister Crowley.

Nor does the remarkable story end with her physical death for, through the mediumship of Margaret Lumley Brown and others, continued contacts with Dion Fortune have been reported over subsequent years.

ISBN 978-1-870450-45-4